Lost and Found

The Forest Chronicles Book 1

Amanda H. Williams

Cover Design: Matthew Steele Hunter
Editor: Carlene Garboden

This is a work of fiction. Names, characters, organizations, places, events, and incidents are products of the author's imagination or are used fictitiously, and any resemblance to actual persons, living or dead, business establishments, events or locales is entirely coincidental.

ISBN: 1530599156
ISBN 13: 9781530599158

ACKNOWLEDGMENTS

All the glory goes to the Lord Jesus Christ for the completion of this project.

A special thanks to Jeromy Williams, my husband and helpmate in life. I love you.
Thank you for your patience and thank you for the laughter.
Thank you to my precious children who have been gifted to us. Zachary and Mackenzie, I simply love you.

Thank you to my readers: Jen, Beth, Shae, Allyson, Carlene, Diana, and Tammy. Thank you for sharing life's most precious commodity—time.

Tracy, God bless! Amanda H. Williams

Books by Amanda H. Williams:

Becoming Visible

Daughter of the King

Maker of the Rain Volume 1

Maker of the Rain Volume 2

Maker of the Rain Volume 3

Maker of the Rain Volume 4 (Release June 2016)

1

The sun had only just dipped below the horizon, saying its goodnight with a magnificent tapestry of pinks, oranges, yellows, and indigos, by the time Ember Rose Bennett rambled down the long, dirt driveway leading to the half-century old, somewhat secluded log cabin. The sky transitioned from day to night much as a symphony obeys its maestro. She found the timing of her arrival strangely appropriate as the sun was setting on one chapter of her life, yet simultaneously rising on another.

Excitement mounting, Ember quickly unfastened her seatbelt and slipped her cramped legs out of the vehicle and planted them on solid ground—land that now bore her name. A laugh escaped her lips as she jogged up the oak steps, not bothered by the zapping of the overhead light wherein insects met their untimely demise. She took out the key and fiddled with the lock for only a second before she stood just inside the doorway hands shaking slightly, eyes darting from one corner of the room to the next—light and momentary—much like a butterfly's dance. Ember took a deep breath, silently promising all the remembrances she would reacquaint herself soon, and made a beeline to her favorite memory-laden spot. A quick flip of a switch found just inside the back wall of the laundry room lit up the screened lanai that promised a crystal clear view of a small but fully stocked lake she remembered fishing in for hours as a child. Her eyes misted, remembering all the life lessons carefully passed down during the baiting and casting of cane fishing poles while sitting on the edge of the water, munching on apple slices and peanut butter sandwiches.

Ember could already smell the aroma of the delicious coffee she would hold in her hands tomorrow morning while observing the wildlife of the Ocala National Forest. Without thinking, her hand fell on the back of the oak rocker. Gently, she set it in motion, imagining her grandfather so vividly, smoking his pipe and craning his neck toward the starry night; tears sprung to her eyes. Bittersweet peace filled her from the tips of her toes to the top of her head. For months, she had dreamt of this moment.

Shaking off the heaviness of yesterdays gone by, her footsteps took her back into the house, and she ran long, slender fingers through her fiery red ponytail as she explored her new home. Emerald green eyes surveyed every detail: the spotless hardwood floors, the original pine walls, the comfortable open living/kitchen space, the charming four bedrooms, and the newly renovated bathroom. Thirteen hundred square feet wasn't much, but to her this efficient space—once belonging to her beloved grandfather, Ransom Bennett— was paradise. The smooth, coolness of the metal railing slid under the palm of her hand as she lightly skipped down the wooden steps to retrieve the few bags she had brought from Jacksonville. Ember pushed the button on the remote to pop the trunk of her faithful Accord and smiled at the nocturnal serenade tickling her ears. As a little girl, she had always loved nighttime in the forest. She and Pops, slathered in a generous coat of bug-spray and armed with flashlights, would explore trails known only to them. Ember never felt fear with Pops, only a sense of wonder and adventure. She looked forward to revisiting places that reminded her of those happy times.

Smiling to herself, she stopped cold and frowned as bright headlights ominously lit up the woods surrounding the property. Deep breaths filled her chest as she tried to calm a gnawing sense of fear. To her knowledge, no living soul knew she was here tonight. Her hands automatically touched the holster hidden underneath her shirt.

The crunching of gravel rang through the night, and she squinted her eyes as the old, red pickup truck came to a stop before everything was bathed in black, lit only by the dim lights emanating from the porch. Her cell phone with the flashlight was sitting on the console of her car, not doing her any service at the moment. All she could make out was a tall, dark-haired man walking towards her; the sight of him rendering her speechless.

A deep, baritone voice interjected itself into the darkness, "Em?"

Ember audibly gasped. No one called her Em except Pops. Her mother and father called her by her middle name, Rose. She preferred Ember, but Pops tagged her with Em ever since she could toddle.

Her stammered response spoke of fear, "I—I'm sorry, but who are you?"

His voice was quick to respond, seemingly intent on setting her at ease. "Aiden. Aiden Steele —I knew your grandfather," he paused. "Can we move up to the porch so we can see?"

Aiden. The teenager that worked for Pops. Vague recollections of the tall, thin boy fishing with Pops down at the lake lingered on the outskirts of her little girl memory. No longer ready to fight or take flight, she led the way up the stairs. When she turned to face him, the cadence of her heart went into triple time, but not from fear. Aiden Steele stood ramrod straight—at least 6' 2'' with coal black hair that curled around his collar and fell over his forehead, coffee-colored eyes, and smooth olive skin. Calculating from memory, he had to be in his early to mid-thirties. Suddenly, she was conscious of her oversized mocha latte-stained t-shirt, yoga pants, and lack of makeup. The flavor from the sub sandwich and sour cream and onion chips combination she had gobbled on the road casually hung out in her mouth, and she was fairly sure she probably had remnants stuck in her teeth. Again, she rubbed her hand through her tangled curls, trying to adjust any that might have gone wildly astray.

In turn, Aiden put his hands in the front pockets of his dark-washed Wrangler jeans, then looked back at his truck as a dog started barking. Apologetically, he said, "Sorry, that's Rusty."

Ember craned her neck to catch a glimpse of his troubled companion.

He looked back at her to reassure, "He's harmless. Just a chocolate lab that hates being solo."

Nervous laughter echoed through the trees.

"I didn't mean to scare you. Your grandfather wrote me a couple of months ago, told me about his condition and informed me he was leaving the place to you. I—knew he was gone, but I wasn't sure when you would arrive." His head looked to the left of the property through fifty yards of brush. "I live next door and saw the headlights. Wanted to check on everything to make sure all was well." He looked down at the deck before meeting her eyes. "Is it?"

The rhythmic cadence of his voice put her in a trance-like state. Her body shivered as she shook her head willing herself to speak. Unconsciously, her arms found themselves wrapped around her waist, warding off a slight chill. "Yes—yes, I'm fine." She inclined her head, looking up into his eyes. "Thanks for checking on me . . . I remember you."

His head shifted, and his dark eyebrows rose in surprise. "Do you?"

She nodded. "Yes, I was young, but I do remember—you fishing with Pops, doing odd jobs. Am I right?"

Aiden shuffled his feet, cleared his throat, and rubbed his forehead, but with a slight nod confirmed her memory. "I should get going. Can I come by tomorrow morning and go over some paperwork with you?"

In response to her open, quizzical look, he continued, "I've managed the property for the last twelve years. I'd like to go through some of the details with you if that's okay."

Ember fidgeted with the diamond stud in her left ear but slowly nodded. "Yes, of course. Coffee at seven? Or is that too early?"

Aiden walked down the steps of the cabin towards his truck but turned back to answer, "Coffee at seven. Perfect."

She called after him, stopping him in his hurried tracks, "You were there, weren't you?"

Slowly, he turned to face her. She could barely make out his expression, but she sensed rather than saw a look of sadness. "Yes, I was there."

❧

An hour later, Ember finally sat down after unpacking the last of her kitchen essentials. The visit from Aiden brought back a flood of memories of times past, times when she followed her grandfather around like a shadow.

Today was a day to remember. The drive from Jacksonville through the forest wasn't long, but it was sufficient to review the highs and lows of her twenty-five years. Ironic that some days she felt thirteen-years-old again, while other days she felt sixty-three.

Thirteen. A lot happened that year of her life. Ember and her parents moved to Jacksonville from Miami when she was in seventh grade. She had very few happy memories of her parents before the move. In fact, most shades of times past were bathed in silence. Her parents' way of coping with their miserable cohabitation was the unending silent treatment—never violence or raised voices, but a quiet that screamed so loud she had to cover her ears. Therefore, she'd learned from a very young age to read facial expressions to gauge the moods of both mother and father. Within months of moving, the remnants of her parents' marriage fell apart. Then, the cacophony of hurt and bitterness broke the impenetrable silence.

Ember, an unwilling participant in a no-holds-barred screech-filled tug-of-war, was miserable. Desperate for normalcy and peace, she prayed God would somehow rescue her from the mayhem. A giant of a man, Ransom Bennett, known to her as Pops, was His answer.

Ember's mother grew up in the foster system, so she had no known maternal grandparents. Her father's mother passed away from cancer when he was a boy, so the only grandparent Ember ever knew was Pops. From her first memory, she held him in her mind as a force to be reckoned with—a kind, gentle, but firm presence in a tumultuous life. Occasionally, her family would visit Pops out in the forest. Mostly, just she and her father. Even then, she was dropped off for a week while Jase Bennett reunited with old friends. Ember, never upset at her father's departure, would follow behind Ransom like an eager puppy, ready to learn whatever life lesson he had on his agenda to teach.

When Pops moved from Ocala to Jacksonville to be a support system for Ember—to be her mother, father, and in many ways, her mentor—Ember felt as if she'd somehow been rescued. He spent time with her, helped her with homework, came to all her track meets, and proudly watched as she graduated from high school and then college. Ember was born with natural confidence; a respectful defiance channeled to rise to the occasion when challenged. Ignored at home, she learned to gain respect through achievement and praise. She would be noticed, even if she had to outperform everyone else to make it happen. Pops carried the wisdom to help mold that energy, which could have been destructive, into something productive and positive.

Soon after graduation, Ember's world changed when her mother moved across the country with her new boyfriend, followed by her father's decision to experience his youth again at the age of fifty—in Miami.

But, Pops, her foundation, remained solid. He was who she went to when she got her first job as a high school English teacher. He was who she went to when everything in her life went topsy turvy. He was who she went to when tragedy punched her in the gut, threatening to paralyze and steal everything she knew.

Suddenly, images of her first love flooded her mind. As a laser-focused teenager and college student, boys were on the peripheral and never tempted her beyond a casual flirtation. As a result, no boy or man had ever touched her heart. She had seen first hand the destructive nature of a marriage forced by consequences of temptation—of which she was the product—and she would wish her childhood on no one. She supposed divorce and a strained relationship built walls, but Pops also provided a standard hard to attain. Then, one encounter, one boy changed it all. Ember put her head on the back of the couch and closed her eyes, allowing herself moments to remember—a luxury her grief counselor encouraged her to savor.

Jonah Emit entered the pages of Ember's life as a superhero. A new teacher at a large public school, Ember was intimidated by the students, the veteran teachers, the administration, and in particular by an intense fear of failure. For the first time in her life, whispers of "what ifs" threatened to paralyze her will to overcome. Jonah, a single rookie math teacher, sat beside her on the first day of orientation. Immediately, his laughter invaded every cell of her being. By the end of week one, he picked her up for their first date. She basked in his confidence, and within a month, the first year jitters had disappeared like early morning mist. Six months later, they were on the verge of something permanent, when a phone call turned her life upside down.

News of blonde hair, blue-eyed Jonah, a math geek that all the students fell in love with, a twenty-two-year-old guy with a sense of humor that would rival any stand-up comedian broke her world. Jonah, who loved Jesus, and served him faithfully; Jonah Emit, breathed his last breath on the side of I-95 when a drunk driver unknowingly aimed his car like a missile on a mission. In an instant, Jonah was gone.

The student body reeled, distraught their teacher had been taken from them. His parents, whom she'd grown to respect, his sisters—all of them were devastated. Ember was numb for months—going through the motions of life, checking off her boxes but disconnecting from any real feeling. She filled her days and nights—unwilling to stop long enough and experience the pain. Leigh, her mother, tried to offer comfort but was so wrapped up in her budding relationship, based in Seattle, with a man half her age, that all hugs and platitudes were as empty as a dry well. Her father attended the funeral, but Jase Bennett had never been a fountain of wisdom. His reflection in the mirror only showed himself, with no room for anyone else, even his only child. As soon as she unlocked the front door of her apartment after the memorial service, her father gifted her with a kiss on the cheek before heading south for Miami. His social life took precedence over his daughter's shattered heart.

Pops was there though. Through months of denial ticking towards grief—the ready shoulders that held her while she cried were those of Pops. The soothing, gentle voice who counseled her through doubt and anger belonged to Pops. The wrinkled, rock solid hands that held the Bible, while praying Scripture over her were those of Pops. She was convinced her broken heart was mended because Pops was her lifeline.

However, her world continued to wobble when three short years later, Pops, her best friend, received the diagnosis that everyone dreads—cancer; that horrible six letter word that robs so many of life.

Saying goodbye to Pops, her beloved grandfather, was the most excruciating phrase she had ever uttered. But she knew if she didn't give him permission to go, he would hang on to this life with every labored breath. She loved him too much to watch him suffer anymore. The memory of sitting beside him in the hospital with his once strong hand, now frail, holding onto hers would never leave her mind. Branded on her soul were his last words, "Em, don't be afraid to love again," his voice crackled, but he continued, "with your whole heart. Trust, baby girl. Seek direction, but don't be afraid to move in the direction you are called and don't be afraid of the silence. Listen. Embrace it and seek wisdom from the only One who has it to give." Her tears soaked the sterile hospital sheets as she leaned close to his mouth. Despite the difficulty of speaking, he was intent on finishing his message, "You will never be alone. Never. Promise me you will remember."

All she could do was nod her head, promising she would try to trust. She would attempt to rest—something he accused her of never doing. According to Pops, she was always trying to prove something to someone—to deserve love. The last words he heard from her trembling lips were the only ones that mattered. "I love you, Pops." Minutes later he was gone. With his last breath, the foundation that she rested on crumbled to ashes. Ember felt—lost.

Both parents showed up for the service, but no looks were exchanged. They went through the motions, flanked on either side of her and then quickly went their separate ways. Again, horrible silence. She remembered looking out over the few people in attendance and seeing a stranger standing on the outskirts of the graveyard. The rain obscured a clear view, but the tall, dark figure retreated before she could find out who he was. Consumed by her grief, and walking through the motions, she forgot about the mysterious appearance—until today. Seeing Aiden shadowed in the front yard evoked the memory from that horrible day. He was there.

Neither parent cared to be present for the reading of the will, neither cared much about Pops as far as she was concerned. Strained on a good day, the relationship between Ransom and his son wavered from tentative to civil. However, the last twelve years had been riddled with constant turmoil, typically around her father's inability to grow up and take responsibility for his choices. The fact that Pop's only possession, outside of the few boxes housed in apartment 316 in the assisted living facility, went to Ember, surprised no one.

The cabin in the forest. The cabin she had only visited a handful of times as a child, before Pops moved and rented it out to outdoorsmen looking for adventure. The cabin where she could hopefully find what was desperately missing from her life, something she could depend on, something she could believe in again. The cabin in the quiet of the woods, where maybe she could befriend the silence, rest in it, instead of running from it.

Spring came, and Ember did not renew her teaching contract. Today, on the last day of post-planning in early June, Ember headed south with a packed car and a heavy heart but with hope for tomorrow.

Aiden carefully navigated the familiar driveway before making an immediate right on his property. Slowly, he put his faithful truck—one he'd fixed up in high school and couldn't bear to part with—in park and cut the lights but didn't get out. Rusty sensed something was wrong because instead of demanding release, he laid his head on Aiden's lap. Absently, Aiden ran his fingers through Rusty's silky dark chocolate coat. He looked down at the dog and released a half laugh, before looking up at the ceiling of his truck. He pulled down the visor where a time-worn picture of him standing next to a large, older man stared back at him. They'd been fishing, and Aiden had snagged the biggest trout he'd caught to date. The expression on Pop's face–priceless—a mixture of indignation at having been out-fished but also an intense pride that still brought tears to his eyes. Aiden spoke through emotion to the picture as if the man himself would respond, "Pops, what are you trying to do to me?"

The old man had been for all essential purposes, his father. A rebellious fifth grader, up to no good, Aiden met his match in Ransom Bennett, a volunteer at the elementary school he attended. Ransom coached tackle football and noticed the unusual aggression boiling over in Aiden. After doing a little research, Ransom apparently learned Aiden's story. Abandoned by an abusive father, being raised by a single mother who worked three jobs, young Aiden ran wild and answered to no one. Ransom took the time to contact his mom and charmed her into allowing him to work with him after school.

Coach Bennett drove him relentlessly on the football field and taught him about effort and motivation, and then the value of a work ethic when he hired him to help him out on the property doing odd jobs. As a full-blown teenager, he invested in Aiden with life's most precious commodity—time. Eventually known to him as "Pops," Aiden knew he owed the old man everything, mainly because Ransom introduced him to faith in Someone beyond himself. Although he had only seen Ransom a handful of times over the last decade, he loved him. He would do anything for him, and Ransom knew that. Aiden had agreed to manage the property when Pops moved to Jacksonville to be with his beloved Ember. And during their last stream of correspondence, Aiden decided to follow through on something he would only do for the man who had invested so much time in him. He agreed to watch over his precious granddaughter.

In his mind's eye, Aiden could visualize the energetic, inquisitive little girl who tagged behind her grandfather the few times he'd seen her. No way he would forget the freckle-peppered fiery, redhead with sparkling eyes the color of evergreen oaks. But Ransom had not shared that the little girl had grown into a stunning beauty—one that had the power in one short conversation to render him speechless. One that he suspected had passion and determination simmering underneath the surface. No, Ransom didn't fill him in on any of that vital information.

Exiting the truck, followed by Rusty, Aiden bypassed the expansive front porch of his renovated farmhouse and marched towards the stables. There, he found Solo and Freedom, the two quarter horses he called friends. Solo, his dark bay horse, was gentle and easy going, whereas Freedom, with her rich, coppery coat, was more adventurous boasting a hint of mischief. As he watered and fed his family, Aiden mentally dug his heels into his lifestyle. He was a loner, a writer—one who had moderate success in the vast world of fiction. He fished, gardened, hunted, canoed, kayaked, and was perfectly satisfied with the solitary existence he had so carefully crafted. Ever since Audrey, he had no desire to nurture relationships, much less one with a beautiful young woman. Five long years had passed since Audrey left him waiting—at the altar. No, Aiden had learned his lesson more than once when it came to loving someone with all your heart. When that someone betrays you, the fallout is unbearable. Walking back to the house with Rusty by his side, he knew what he would say to Ember tomorrow. He had a plan, one that did not include her as a neighbor.

Ember chose the largest bedroom with the picture window facing the right side of the property. As she closed the last drawer in the antique oak chest, she was satisfied with her progress for the evening. Besides the kitchen and bathroom necessities, she had only packed clothes and a few pictures; she had no desire to change anything about her little haven. She would have to drive into Ocala to pick up a few essentials the next day, but overall she was set. As she lay in bed reading a new best-selling novel, she took a moment to thank God for the blessing of safe travel and for bringing her to these crossroads in her life.

The wall of crosses, the arrangement untouched through the years, drew her attention. Pops and the grandmother she'd never met collected them through the years. Some were simple and others more elaborate; they all reminded her that Jesus stretched out His arms on the cross for everyone, regardless of what they looked like or where they came from–a fact she was ever so grateful to embrace. Pops introduced her to the Jesus, who welcomed little children instead of silencing them when she was eight years old. Through the ups and downs, her faith grew from a tiny seed to one that propelled her forward. She learned, even in the face of loss and pain, hope existed. Pops helped her navigate through the crises of faith in the face of all she'd been through, and in her heart of hearts, she knew Jesus would meet her right where she was. Her heart still hurt from so many losses and the insecurities she'd experienced as a child and nurtured as an adult—insecurities that had to be surrendered every single day. Part of her still believed she had to prove herself, prove her worth, even prove she could start over again. But she was determined to stop believing the lies, she was determined to embrace hope.

The chiseled face of Aiden Steele floated through her mind. Aiden. The essence of pain hardened his gaze when he looked at her during their earlier conversation, yet there was something else in that look too. Something she couldn't identify.

Property manager. No wonder the meticulously kept surrounding acre and the fifty-year-old cabin appeared brand-new. Even the outlying shed was well taken care of from what she could tell. Was it possible that he loved her grandfather as she had? Was it possible they might share their sorrow? Ember blinked rapidly and attempted to refocus on the descriptive words laying across her lap beckoning her to escape into the story. She didn't have time to focus on Aiden. She was here to stand on her own two feet, to learn to live independently—a new home, a new job, a new community, a new start. After all, the memory of Jonah was real and reminded her firsthand, the pain associated with love lost.

2

The next morning, Aiden methodically went through his morning ritual of rising before dawn and drinking his first cup of black coffee while reading his devotional. Usually, he would run the three-mile trail behind his house before returning to write, uninterrupted for at least two hours. However, today held a different activity. Today, he would walk next door and talk to Ember, discover her plan, and hopefully reinforce her idea of looking at this cabin as an investment, not a home. Aiden grabbed the file of paperwork that held precise records of the upkeep and maintenance of the cabin and chose to walk on the rough path through the brush to her property instead of the hop, skip, jump drive. Rusty, barking discontentedly, wasn't happy to be left alone in the house, but Aiden didn't want the distraction this morning. He had to get down to business and leave no room for discussion or argument.

Honestly, after mulling over the situation during a toss and turn evening, he didn't know what Ransom was thinking leaving the acre lot with the log cabin to his granddaughter. What did she know about living in the forest? Hadn't she lived in the city all her life? Bottom line, it wasn't safe, and he intended to tell her. She could sell it or rent it out with no problem whatsoever. The property backed up to the hundred-mile equestrian trail, and the cabin was a prime location for any outdoorsman as indicated by the consistent booking of the place since Ransom's departure. Aiden, willing and able to continue property management, would make it easy for her by presenting the facts in a way that would brook no argument from any reasonable person. She could continue to collect an income—and even draw from the healthy savings sustained through years of Pop's discipline—to afford something in town. No, there would be no room for argument. He'd promised to protect her, but he didn't have time to babysit. Aiden, determined to make her understand, rapped on the metal framed screened door.

Ember woke to a rapping sound. Where was she? Her eyes popped open, taking in the pine walls—one wall on the opposite side of the room held a childhood favorite of hers—an old Thomas Kinkade entitled *Living Waters*. The tendrils of sleep faded away, and she glanced to the right out the side window. Trees, lots of trees. The forest . . . Aiden! She quickly threw back the patchwork quilt and swung her legs over the side of the queen-sized bed and glanced at the time on her phone. 7:01 a.m. Rolling her eyes, she chided herself for sleeping late. She never did that! Quickly throwing on shorts and a tank-top, she brushed her teeth and frowned at her wild bed head. No time now. At least she had taken her makeup off the night before and didn't have mascara smeared down her face. She ran to the door and flung it open, apology poised on her lips when the sight of the man on the other side of the entry rendered her speechless. He was more beautiful in the light of day than in the dark of night. He looked freshly showered with khakis and a royal blue collared shirt. Brown, almost black eyes instantly processed and understood the situation but chose to say nothing. Finally, his quirked eyebrow and reluctant but amused gaze focused on her blushing face.

"I'm so sorry, Aiden. Obviously, I slept late." She opened the door and motioned him in. "Please, make yourself at home. I'll put on a pot of coffee. It shouldn't take long."

Self-conscious, but determined to remain somewhat poised, she turned her back and busied herself in the galley kitchen. Any other morning she would have set her coffee for an automatic brew that in and of itself would wake her up. But last night, exhaustion set in, and the task never got accomplished. She poured water into the carafe and measured out the beans in the grinder. Within seconds, the sweet sound and smell of coffee brewing set her mind at ease.

Turning to Aiden, who sat on the couch looking through paperwork, she asked, "Do you mind if I freshen up while this is brewing?"

Briefly, without focusing on her, he nodded his head and flicked a hand in her direction. "Go ahead. No problem."

Aiden had heard the door to the bathroom close before he exhaled. Never had he reacted to a woman in such a way. Ember's rolled out of bed appearance put his heartbeat in overtime. Her illustrious, red curls were pulled back last night; in the light of day, the sunlight moved through her fiery mane that had been set free in slumber, making her appear as if she was an angel sent straight from the gates of heaven. What was wrong with him? Had it been that long since he reacted to a beautiful woman? Five years. Maybe he did need to get out more.

Ember brushed on a light coat of lip gloss and mascara. Her shoulder-length curls had a mind of their own this morning, and it would take more time than she had to attempt to tame them. Exiting the bathroom and finding Aiden in the same spot, intensely focused on the folder spread open on the square coffee table, she swiftly moved to the kitchen. "What do you take in your coffee?"

He didn't look up, only grumbled, "Black is fine."

She quirked an eyebrow at his tone but nodded as she poured a cup for him, then moved to fill her favorite mug with french vanilla creamer, a shot of peppermint, and the steaming black liquid. Taking both in her hands, she walked toward him and carefully handed one over.

He took it from her and sipped it. His eyes, lit up with pleasure, looked at her with newfound appreciation. "This is good." He took another sip. "Really good."

"Thanks. I love a good cup of coffee. It's one of my many weaknesses."

Apparently a man of few words, he took another sip, and she guessed he expected her to sit. She had other ideas.

Ember looked longingly towards the back of the house and asked, "Do you mind if we move to the back porch?"

Something in his eyes told her he did mind. Nevertheless, good manners propelled him off the couch with the folder tucked underneath his arm. Ember sat in Pop's chair, legs drawn up underneath her chin and reveled in the aroma that was tickling her nose. She breathed deep and rested in the view, slowly rocking back and forth, appreciating the quiet of the morning. Aiden took a seat in the other rocking chair. He looked out at the lake for a while. Then, she could sense his eyes on her—waiting. She met his gaze, somewhat embarrassed. "Sorry. I've dreamt of this moment for a long time." Caught off guard, she blinked the tears away and took a sip of coffee to wash down the emotion swelling in her throat.

Aiden's eyes squinted, crinkling the edges. The sunlight brought her attention to the few gray strands woven through his black hair which only added to his overall appeal. "What do you mean?"

Her eyes examined his face. She caught herself wondering about his heritage if he had Native American in his bloodlines. "About what?"

"Dreaming of this moment."

"Since Pops passed and I found out he left this piece of heaven to me—let's just say I've been itching for this morning to become my new normal."

Aiden's eyebrows hit his hairline, and his deep voice went up a notch. A piece of heaven? "You mean to stay?"

Ember put the coffee cup down on the table and stared at him, not anticipating the questioning of her residence. "Of course, I mean to stay. Did you expect me to leave?"

He huffed and raked his fingers through his hair. "Well, yes. I mean I figured you would sell or lease it. I didn't expect you to live here."

Ember's eyebrows crinkled in confusion. "Why ever not?"

"First, it isn't safe for a woman your age—"

Ember felt her defenses rise. "What does my age have to do with it? I'm not a child."

"I know you're not a child—"

"Then what is your point?"

Electricity, tension, and physical attraction brewed in the air like a storm.

Aiden got up and put his hands in his pockets, pacing the length of the lanai. He stared at the water, before turning to her. He looked exotic, with his straight nose and full lips complemented by his dark skin. If the storm on his face wasn't in a full gale, he would be extremely handsome. "Em . . ."

Again, her heart sped up at the use of her grandfather's pet name.

He kneaded his right shoulder as if this conversation was causing him an exorbitant amount of stress. Finally, he stopped and faced her, waving his arms in both directions. "What do you know about living in the forest? I mean, it's remote. You are quite a few miles from town in either direction. There are wild animals out here. Believe it or not, the forest has quite an ominous reputation."

She started laughing, provoking a stern frown. Sitting up, she stared straight into his face, unblinking, and attempted to maintain a serious expression. "Aiden, this isn't the wild west in the nineteenth century. It is 2016. I am capable of taking care of myself. I'm armed with an automobile, lots of technology, and a gun. A lethal combination in any setting."

"A gun?"

"Yes, Pops also taught me how to shoot when I was younger. I'm always packing, and I rarely miss."

Aiden sat back in his chair and took a swig of his coffee. He sat it back down on the table before asking, "What will you do for a living?"

By his tone, she guessed he thought that question would stump her. Insulted, she rolled her eyes. As if she would move to a new place without a plan. "I'm a high school English teacher, and I have already secured a position at Springs High. Are you familiar with that school?"

Eyes widened in surprise; he unsuccessfully tried to cover his shock. "Of course, I am. It's where most of the kids in the forest go—I went there." The last part was mumbled as if she wasn't supposed to hear it.

Apparently, he wasn't expecting for her to set up hearth and home because he sat back in his chair somewhat defeated. She wondered what she had done to cause him not to want her here. Did Pops pay him to manage the property? Was she robbing him of income?

"If this is about you managing the property, I certainly didn't mean to take away income—"

His face turned sharply towards hers. "Excuse me?"

She finished off her coffee and shrugged her shoulders. "There has to be some reason you don't want me here. Is it the money?"

"Absolutely not. Well, he did pay me for the first year, but afterward, I wouldn't take it. Not after I—Pops hasn't paid me in over a decade. I did—I do it— because I . . ."

She finished his sentence without thinking, "Because you loved him?"

Aiden's long fingers curled around the handle of his cup. He nodded slightly.

"What do you do for a living?"

"I'm a writer."

Curiosity crossed her face. She didn't want to pry, but she was an avid reader, a lit major, and an English teacher. The question was inevitable. "What kind of writer?"

"Fiction. Novels."

"Would I—"

He cut her off by standing hastily, causing her near whiplash. She started to get up, but the rushed, terse staccato of words halted her. "Don't get up. Enjoy your morning. Thank you for the coffee. I have to go. I'm going to leave the information with you. Please ask if you have questions. I'll be glad to answer them." He looked at her with a resigned expression before adding, "If you need anything, Em, just let me know."

And with that, he was gone.

Later that afternoon, Aiden's eyes looked up from the computer screen and abandoned the blank page, frustrated by his lack of progress. A scene set on one of Georgia's beautiful border islands halted hours ago, the conveyer belt of words coming to a resounding stop. The sound of some lawn equipment drew his attention to the window that overlooked Ransom's—Ember's—property. Through the brush, he could see a sliver of someone trimming the hedges surrounding the cabin. Curiosity, known for killing cats, was the lifeline of writers—even shy, reclusive ones. Signaling Rusty, Aiden opened up the front door to his farmhouse. For a moment, he simply stood and admired the setting in which he lived. Constructed in the 1800s, the old homestead breathed history, and Aiden inhaled it every single day he was blessed to live here. His life had certainly taken some unexpected twists and turns landing him back in the place in which he grew up.

After college, he stayed home for a year, trying to decide what he was going to do with his life. Ransom's plan to go to Ember was set in motion, and he automatically offered the cabin to Aiden for a year in exchange for him keeping the place up. A series of events led him to an internship with a travel magazine, which led him on a trek across the United States. Technology and local connections enabled his management of the property. During his travels, Aiden wrote about location and setting, with the aim of attracting tourists like bees to honey. It eventually parlayed into writing a novel that to his surprise caught the attention of an agent and eventually a publisher. Amazement continued as they all watched in awe as it shot to the best-seller list six years ago.

Aiden's heart yearned to be settled into some place of his own. His mother had remarried to a solid, good man, and he could have lived with them temporarily, but he wasn't wired that way. He had seen the country, encountered more people—good and bad—than he ever wanted to, completed journal after journal, character study after character study. He just wanted to be, to live on his land, and to write. He had always dreamed of buying something old and fixing it up while maintaining its integrity. This old house he grew up in the shadow of seemed the perfect fit. Abandoned for years, Ransom used to tell him stories about the original owners from decades past. Aiden spent many hours playing in the dilapidated building, but with a lot of blood, sweat and many tears coupled with a healthy savings account and a decent advancement, he was able to make it into something beautiful.

Every board, every drop of paint, every fixture reflected a journey he took that eventually brought him to his knees. Audrey didn't sit beside him at the closing; in fact, the week after their "wedding" he signed the final papers. It was supposed to be the ultimate gift—a surprise. Aiden paused and looked back at the house. It represented so much to him, but mostly it represented a haven where every nook and every cranny didn't remind him of the woman with whom he fell in love. She'd never even laid eyes on it, preferring town to the forest. He wondered now why he ever thought she would agree to live here. It was a testament to his state of denial.

Their relationship had not been perfect; in fact, many that knew them were shocked they made five years. He met Audrey Ludelle at church. She was lovely, with flaxen hair and cornflower blue eyes. Tall and willowy next to his stature, they seemed to be a perfect fit.

They shared their faith and some of the same hopes and dreams, but their temperaments were almost too similar. Audrey was placid, so much so at times, he wanted to shake her to get a reaction. She whole-heartedly agreed with most of his suggestions, but deep down, he knew she had reservations. Instead of voicing them, she kept them hidden in places forbidden to him. He didn't understand it, and the constant solving of her puzzle wore him out in places he would never admit. Aiden loved his fiancee. He even missed her. At times, he ached for her calming presence. But, if he were honest with himself, there was always something missing. Neither was brave enough to voice their concerns, but when the moment of truth defined by her first step down the aisle arrived, she couldn't take it. Apparently, just like in the movies, she ran away. A letter brought to him by a mortified bridesmaid explained her heart, something she couldn't do in person. Much too late, standing in front of five hundred of their closest family and friends, he learned she felt trapped and needed freedom. She not only left him, but she left the country—ran away from home and him. Two years ago, her mother conjured up the courage to call and tell him that Audrey married another man, a fellow traveler, and they now lived out West. The life he was supposed to have belonged to someone else.

Suddenly noticing Rusty's absence, he heard Ember's enthusiastic voice next door. No more buzzing lawn equipment, only a melody of notes that seemed to cause the breeze to blow and the memory-laden sadness to lift a little. Carefully, Aiden walked through the few yards of brush that separated their homes. The vision that met his eyes took his breath away.

Ember, simply dressed in cut-offs, a tank top, a ball cap and tennis shoes knelt down and gave Rusty the affection for which he begged. It felt like reverse déjà vu—something he hadn't experienced, yet would—someday. The hedge trimmer lay forgotten on the grass beside her for the moment. Upon seeing him, she stood up and brushed off her knees. "Hi. Hope I wasn't bothering you," she motioned to the equipment. "I know it's loud." With that statement, he left her sparkling eyes long enough to notice the earbuds hanging from her creamy, white shoulders.

"You weren't bothering me." Outright lie. "I needed to get up and stretch for a bit." His gaze swept the hedges around the house. "I can do this for you, or I can hire someone."

Her small, straight, freckle-peppered nose crinkled in response. "No need. I know how to operate the machinery, and I enjoy the work. I drove into town and picked up some planters and bulbs I want to place around the exterior."

Aiden nodded his head thoughtfully and examined a bird soaring above them in the powder blue sky before speaking the words he'd been thinking about all day, "I'm sorry about earlier. I didn't mean to imply that I didn't want a neighbor. It's just that . . ."

Ember held up one finger and casually touched his shoulder. "Hold that thought. Do you want some water?"

Aiden, shocked at being cut off, stood speechless as she pivoted and ran up the steps of the porch. Within seconds, she was back, handing him a plastic bottle. It was impossible for him to look away as he watched her turn up the contents of the entire container in one long gulp. She wiped her mouth with the back of her hand. "Sorry, I was getting a little woozy. What were you saying?"

Visions of her fainting in front of him and being the one to catch her drove him to distraction. Maybe he'd dwelled in the land of fiction for too long. "I was just apologizing for earlier. The way I left was rude. Especially on such a special morning—one you had been looking forward to. I feel like I made a dream into a nightmare, and for that, I'm truly sorry."

She brushed his arm with her hand, and then pulled away suddenly. Did she feel the same sensation he did? Maybe he needed to drink his water. "It's okay. You're no scary monster lurking in the closet or under the bed. Knowing Pops, he probably made you promise to look out for me, didn't he?"

Aiden, taken aback by her perception, shook his head. "No, he didn't make me. He asked me to look out for you, and I told him I would."

Ember bit her bottom lip that drew his attention to her rose-colored lips. Lips that he suddenly wanted to kiss. What was wrong with him?

"So you agreed?"

All he could do was nod.

She shook her head, and as she did, several red curls escaped their confinement and landed gracefully on her bare neck. "Pops meant well, Aiden. I have no doubt. And . . . I know you loved him too. But please, don't feel obligated to me. I'm twenty-five and have lived a little. Like I said, I know how to take care of myself. I don't need the babysitting, and I certainly don't want to be an added burden."

She was giving him an out, one that he wanted. Or did he? The idea of her independence was a relief to him, but what if he didn't want to leave her alone. They were neighbors, after all.

Ember continued, "However, I could use a friend. I know no one here. Not one soul, except for the principal who offered me the position." She paused, apparently trying to read his facial expressions, "So, what do you say?" Em's hand reached out towards him.

Without thinking, he took it and the warmth of her touch nearly knocked him off his feet. "I'd like that, Em. Friends."

3

Aiden, shirtless in plaid pajama pants, drinking his first cup of coffee and perusing the headlines on his iPad, startled at the sudden knock on his door. He looked at the time. 6:00 a.m. Ember. Quickly, he took two strides to reach the entryway, afraid she might be in trouble. His concern faded when he opened the door to her smiling, albeit embarrassed expression. His expression must have communicated his confusion as he stood looking at her, dressed in running shorts, a matching t-shirt and ball cap combination with bright pink cursive writing spelling out the message, *Just Bless It.* She was armed with earbuds and a strapped on iPhone, bright-eyed and full of energy.

She winced and laughed nervously. "Aiden, I saw the light. I hope I'm not interrupting. I'm sorry it's so early, but I noticed the path behind your house. I like to run in the mornings and . . ." He watched as she took in his night time attire and was somewhat amused at the blush spreading across her neck and face.

Aiden stepped to the right to motion her inside. "It's a three-mile trail, and you are welcome to run it . . . but I would prefer if you wouldn't do it alone."

In the span of two blinks, she stood awkwardly in the hallway staring at him, finally saying, "Aiden, I am perfectly—"

He held up his hand in protest. "I'm sure you are, but Em, they don't call this the forest for nothing. I run that path every morning, and I'll be glad to go with you. But there are real, live animals in those woods."

Ember shrugged, nonchalantly. "Of course, there are animals." She paused as if processing the possibilities. "What—like snakes and raccoons and stuff?"

"And bears, gators, deer, turkeys . . ."

"Bears?" Ember's voice went up a notch, and his mind flashed back to the adorable freckle-faced eight-year-old. She was cute, if a little naive.

"Yes, bears. Did you notice all the bear signs driving here the other evening? They even have a byway named after them. That reminds me—you need to read that travel book I left in the kitchen for guests. It has helpful information about separating trash to avoid bears. Besides, occasionally there are even people out there."

"People?"

"There are groups of people, some campers or wildlife enthusiasts looking to connect with nature, others who don't have a house to call home. People flock to the forest for various reasons. Most are harmless; some are not. I don't often see them, but I have on occasion."

Silence followed by a whisper, "Oh."

"Tell you what, I run every morning. In fact, I was finishing up my coffee and was about to change. What do you say we run it together?" He was already climbing the staircase beside the front door.

Her voice rose as she looked at his retreating figure, "I don't want to cramp your style."

Under his breath, clear of her ears, he muttered, "Way too late for that." However, he couldn't erase the smile poised on his lips.

Ember recovered from the sight of Aiden first thing in the morning and stood open-mouthed as she looked at her surroundings. The exterior view of the quaint farmhouse, complete with stone chimney and sparkling white wrap around porch, sat peacefully in the center of Aiden's land, pleasant and unassuming. The interior was nothing short of magazine worthy and spectacular. The dark-paneled yellow-southern pine walls and ceiling looked to be original, along with the rough-cut ash hardwood floors. Aiden's decor, in a few words—rugged, minimalistic, functional, and masculine. Ember didn't leave the entryway but noticed what promised to be the hint of a spacious kitchen with a large, wooden farm table in the back of the house. A long hallway flowed through the middle, flanked by several rooms to the right and left.

Soon, Aiden bounded down the stairs, dressed in running attire.

He reached over and lightly touched the earphones hanging around her neck. "Leave those here, okay."

"Oh," she removed them. "Do you like to talk while you run?"

Aiden's laugh was a low rumble, one that warmed her down deep inside. "To myself? No. I don't run with music because I want to be aware of what and who is around me. You should too."

Feeling very junior highish, Ember placed the phone and earbuds on the repurposed entryway table he was tapping on as he spoke.

"Ready?"

Ember nodded enthusiastically, suddenly desperate to expend pent-up energy that seemed to be electric when confined in a closed space with him. "Yep."

She followed him down the long, narrow hallway. Ember noticed an office, a living space, a dining room, and a spare bedroom on the bottom floor and then she took in the full disclosure of the kitchen. Aiden wasn't stopping for her perusal, but rough-hewed beams with a variety of metals and stonework reminded her of an episode straight from one of her favorite HGTV shows, *This Old House.*

Aiden walked through the back door, down the concrete steps, and faced the entrance to the trail.

Ember followed his lead and began stretching. "Did you carve this out or has it always been here? I don't remember it."

Aiden looked up from the ground. “I carved out the trail shortly after I finished the house. I’ve always enjoyed running but don’t necessarily want to drive to a track to do it.”

Ember nodded, wondering how often the seemingly private man left his property.

She jumped up and down to get her blood flowing. “I don’t want to slow you down, Aiden. Please go at your normal pace,” she pleaded.

His hand lightly brushed her shoulder. “Come on, Em. We’ll be fine.”

And they were. Their pace was a comfortable nine-minute mile, perfect for a morning run. Ember kept her eye out for anything unusual, but so far all she heard was a lot of early morning bird calls. About a mile into their run, Aiden warned softly, “Watch out for some of these roots. It can get a little bumpy.”

She nodded her head, willing herself to be careful. She did not want to fall flat on her face in front of him. Soon, they reached a tree that had 1.5 carved into the bark. Aiden looped around it and ran back toward the farmhouse. “We’re making good time. You feeling okay?”

She smiled—winded, but able to speak. “Yes. Perfect. Thanks for doing this with me. I should be okay from here on out, Aiden.”

He didn’t respond, and she wasn’t quite sure why. Soon, they arrived in his backyard, and Ember found herself pumped full of endorphins ready to tackle the day. Between heavy breaths, she thanked him. They both took a few moments to stretch. Not quite knowing what to say, she whispered, “Well, thanks again, Aiden. I’ll—”

“Em?”

She looked back over her shoulder and tried to revel in the joy evoked by the hint of a smile gracing his handsome face. “Your phone?”

Embarrassed, she laughed lightly. “Pops always said I’d forget my head if it weren’t glued to my shoulders.”

"Sounds like him," Aiden commented as he turned toward the house.

Ember's heart responded to the sadness in his voice. It was then that she knew Aiden must miss her grandfather tremendously. Words of comfort were poised on her lips but froze there upon seeing his posture. Aiden seemed like such a private person, not openly rude, but guarded.

They entered the kitchen through the backdoor, and again Ember was awestruck at how much the man in front of her mirrored his home. She watched as he opened the teal, distressed cabinetry to bring out two old-fashioned glass mason jars. He walked to the refrigerator, topped off two glasses of ice water, and handed one to her. Gratefully, she drank. She gently placed the glass down on the matching island. "Your home is spectacular, Aiden."

He moved to place the two glasses in the sink, looked back at her, and lifted his shoulder in a modest half shrug. "Thank you. It was a lot of hard work, but I'm happy with it."

"Did you do it all yourself?"

Eyes downcast, he nodded.

She looked around the kitchen, her voice holding a hint of awe. "Do you even enjoy cooking?"

Again, Aiden's deep laughter met her ears as he brushed the palm of his hand across the table, wiping away imaginary crumbs. "I do. Why?"

Her voice rose a notch, teasing, "It would be almost sinful for you to be the owner of this kitchen if you didn't use it."

Aiden turned his head sideways, considering her words. "I'll take that as a compliment."

"Good, it was meant to be one. Have you always known how to refinish and repurpose things? This must have been quite a project. Who taught you?"

The previous sadness in his tone found his eyes, and she immediately knew the answer. Pops. Aiden moved down the hallway towards the front door.

A sick feeling came over Ember. She didn't know Aiden's story, but she had a feeling Pops moving to Jacksonville left a great big hole in his life. All because of her. He must hate her.

Ember slowly picked up her phone and earbuds, and tucked them into her shorts pocket. Aiden stood looking at her, seemingly unsure of what to say. "Aiden, I–" And then the words poured out over one another, "I'm sorry for taking him from you."

Aiden's heart flipped over in his chest at her apology. He had enjoyed running with her, spending time with her although no real exchange of words had taken place. Ember seemed comfortable in the silence, and he appreciated that. She seemed genuine. After the debacle with Audrey, he didn't enjoy the company of any woman uncomfortable in her skin. Ember seemed to know herself well and exuded confidence.

He'd never thought of her "taking Pops." True, he missed the old man when he relocated. He needed his mentor more than ever, but he kept in touch with Pops through correspondence—even went to visit through the years. He knew Pops loved him, but he also knew Pops had confidence that the foundation Aiden stood on would be enough to get him started, even if he was fully aware of Aiden's missteps along the way. However, he did not have that same confidence when it came to Em.

Impulsively, Aiden reached out and touched Ember's cheek, much as he pictured Ransom would have done if he could have. The softness of her skin surprised him, and the paternal, or brotherly feelings vanished at his first touch. His hand dropped to his side, but his words were sincere. "Em, don't ever think that. Did I miss him? Of course.

But I was gone the majority of the time by the time he left, and you needed him. And he needed to be there for you. He wanted to be there for you." Watching her tear up, he moved aside as she slowly walked towards the door.

When she crossed the threshold and stepped onto the front porch, now lit softly by the early morning sun, she turned. One lone tear trickled down that same cheek hc had touched. He ached to touch it again, but his hand, fingers stretched out to help forget the electricity of her touch, hung by his side. "Thank you, Aiden. You're right. He saved my life, more than once."

4

The week passed in a blur. Ember spent her time nesting into her new home and acclimating herself to her surroundings. She rarely saw her neighbor, with the exception of their early morning runs. Ember had taken several trips over to the school—eerily quiet during early summer—to prepare for the upcoming school year, and before she knew it, Saturday was here. The two friends followed their routine and sprinted into the backyard when Aiden surprised her with a question.

"What's on your agenda today, Em?"

She shrugged her shoulders. "Not much, just some chores. Why?"

He looked down at the ground and kicked the dirt with his shoe, reminding her of an insecure boy in high school, which surprised her because he was anything but that.

"Are you up for exploring some of the springs today? We could go canoeing and swimming." He looked up at the cloudless sky, eyes crinkling at the brightness of the sun. "It's going to be a beautiful day."

Excitement rose in Ember's gut. Nothing sounded better and more exhilarating than exploring the famous springs she had researched but never visited. "I can be ready in fifteen minutes."

He laughed at her enthusiasm. "All right, then. I'll drive over and pick you up. I just need to get a few things ready."

Twenty minutes later, Ember bounded down the stairs as Aiden pulled up in his red truck; much to her excitement an old, but sturdy canoe and paddles were strapped to the back.

She hopped in, ponytail in full swing with her bag slung over her arm.

Aiden gave her a sideways glance before asking, "Are you all ready?"

Aiden's breath hitched in his throat when Ember's smile of a response lit up the cab. He simply couldn't help himself when the invitation came flying out of his mouth this morning. He had purposefully avoided her this week, but his mind, occupied with the knowledge of her proximity, refused to cooperate. His editor was all over him, asking for the final edits of his latest manuscript. It was due to release at the end of the summer, and then in October he would embark on a month-long book tour making its way out West. Marketing organized a launch team who agreed to spread the release date of his book all over social media, along with teasers to entice buyers, but he had failed to contact them for details. Deadlines were passing him left and right, and all he could do was look out his window trying to catch a glimpse of that wild mane and energetic gait.

"So, where are we going?" Em's voice startled him, and he jolted in his seat.

Embarrassed at being caught swimming with thoughts of her, he quickly cleared his throat. "I thought we'd go to Juniper Springs and do the Juniper Run. It's about seven miles long, but the natural beauty of the forest is worth the exercise."

Em smiled, almost jumping up and down in her seat with excitement.

Aiden thought about all the times he did this run alone, especially after Audrey. Sometimes he would spend whole days in the forest—reading, taking notes, thinking. Today promised to be a better day.

Within an hour, they were launched and navigating the waterway. He was surprised at how well Em did, considering her confession she had only canoed a couple of times. Juniper Springs wasn't the easiest of runs, but she followed direction well. Although she was distracted by the wildlife and dense canopy that at times, made him feel like they were cut off from the rest of the world, he couldn't blame her. The beauty of the forest could be hypnotic.

Silence accompanied them for many minutes before Ember made a statement that succeeded in freezing his paddle. "This suits you. The quiet, the natural beauty, the solitude."

Paddle met water again, but several seconds passed before he answered, "Yes, it does, I suppose." He pointed to a tiny beach to the right. "Let's pull up on that stretch of land and have a snack. What do you say?"

Her ponytail bobbed up and down like an occupied fishing bobber. "Sounds good."

Soon, they beached the canoe, carefully placing the paddles side by side. Aiden took his pack off and brought out two bottles of water, two apples, and a couple of peanut butter and jelly sandwiches.

Ember laughed. "Thank you for thinking of this. It would have been a long day with nothing to go on but the oatmeal I had early this morning."

Aiden dug into his meal, listening to the sounds of the forest, savoring the moment. A memory floated through his mind like an unexpected breeze. He was fifteen years old, and he and Pop had taken this same run. They pulled up on this very beach to rest; the vivid memory taking root somewhere deep down inside. Pops' voice filtered through his head.

"A man's word is the only thing standing at the end of the day, the anchor keeping him on the right course." Ransom looked over at the gangly teenager beside him, "Do you know what I mean by that, Son?"

Aiden looked sideways at the old man, not quite knowing where this was going. He picked up a smooth stone and threw it into the water. "I guess."

"Don't guess about something that important. Ain't rocket science. When you say you're going to do something, then you do it. If you say you're going to stick, then stick."

Teenage angst laced his question, "Is this about me not showing up yesterday?" One of the guys from his class asked him to go to the springs and swim; Aiden skipped out on work, had a miserable time because of the guilt, and showed up the next day tail between his legs. Instead of the punishment or lecture he expected would be waiting for him, Pops had the canoe ready to go when he showed up. This "talk" is what he had anticipated.

Ransom moved to face the boy that was quickly turning into a man but had so much more to learn. He put both hands on Aiden's shoulders and looked straight through his pupils into his soul. "Yes, but it's about so much more than that. It's about being a man, a man of honor. Integrity, character, following through on commitments." Aiden remembered the passion in Ransom's voice, almost like he was trying to teach something he himself had missed the first time.

Aiden looked down at the dirt before having the courage to look in the beloved old man's eyes. "I do understand." And he did. He got it. Ransom presented the picture of what to be—the man that helped bring him into existence was the opposite. Aiden would do anything not to turn into the latter.

His earliest memory was looking up from a coloring book and then quickly finding himself standing between his father's fist and his mother's gut, vividly recollecting the look of horror and resignation on his father's face as he felt his mother's arm shield him from any blows. He watched his father's back exit the house that day and never return. He watched his mother work herself into the ground trying to run away from past mistakes and make a life for him.

Sometimes, Aiden felt the weight of the world on his shoulders, intensified by a compulsion to see the world in black and white—not gray. Throughout his childhood and adult life, Aiden had witnessed all versions of humanity, and he and God struggled many times over wrongs seemingly unpunished.

Fast forward to today and the commitment he made to Pops sat munching on her apple beside him. Ember represented his love for Ransom—all that the old man taught him wrapped into one red-headed package. Part of retreating from the world after Audrey's abandonment was escaping the hurts caused by others. Not risking his heart one more time just to be let down. Ember, in many ways, scared him to death. But he wouldn't let Pops down; he would follow through on what he said. Her voice brought his memory to an end.

"Where'd you go?"

He threw a stick in the water. "Thinking about Pops."

Her green eyes immediately filled with tears. "Me too. I was just thinking about how he would have loved this place."

"He did love this place."

She searched his face. "He brought you here?"

Aiden absently began arranging a variety of sticks into a pile that lay between them. "Yeah, he's the first person, well, actually the only person, besides—"

Her eyebrows rose in question.

Aiden's heart beat rapidly in his chest. Should he tell her about Audrey? Eventually, she would find out. Was he ready for this?

"I was engaged."

A small gasp. "When?"

"Five years ago."

"What happened?"

Aiden got up and began collecting the trash. "She left me." That may have been the first time he voiced the three words of truth that hurt him the most. He was left alone. Abandoned.

Suddenly, a soft hand stopped his movement. His gaze found hers and instead of being angry at the sympathy in her eyes, he was profoundly moved by it.

Her voice was soft, just above a whisper. "I'm sorry."

It wasn't her fault, but somehow just hearing those words from someone who didn't know Audrey helped. He couldn't explain it, but a deep part of him healed at that moment.

He covered her hand with his own. "Thank you. Are you ready?"

"Yes."

Eventually, they returned to the launching point and loaded the canoe on the truck. Aiden took a few twists and turns through the woods before they landed in a parking lot.

"Where are we?" Ember asked.

Aiden got out of the truck and began throwing stuff into his bag. "I told you. We're going swimming. Follow me."

Ember followed Aiden down a short path to a booth where he paid a minimal fee. Steps later she was staring at the most beautiful swimming hole she had ever seen. The water was an indescribable shade of blue-green but clear to the bottom. Water oaks stood majestically guarding the spot. A small stone bridge served as a jumping off point for those who wanted a little adventure. What looked like an old millhouse stood behind it all with trails flanking both sides. Aiden watched, seemingly trying to read her reaction. She had no words as she settled her small bag on a picnic table. Inhibitions forgotten, sheer excitement consumed her, and soon she was laughing and jumping into the middle of the picturesque canvas.

Aiden heard himself laugh and realized he'd done more of that in the last week than he had in years. Watching her dive in and out of the springs, jumping off the bridge, and floating on her back caused the bleakness of his world to transform slowly from black and white to shades of technicolor. He whispered a prayer of thanksgiving before joining her in the fun.

5

Ember woke up the next morning feeling restless. Sunday. She wanted to go to church but had no idea where to attend. Maybe Aiden could point her in the right direction, any direction. Yesterday, in many ways was magical for her. He was still closed off, but yet there was a connection made. Having a friend, one that she could trust and most importantly one who shared the memory of Pops, meant so much to her. Ember could see it all on his face yesterday. Aiden missed Pops in a place not open to her—yet. However, knowing that Pops had a part in shaping this man who she knew deep down inside was a man worth knowing, warmed her.

Still early, the sun was just making its stunning appearance for the day. Ember walked next door with all intentions of asking Aiden if he was up for a run; she would inquire about church then. Climbing through the brush, she heard the faint echo of Aiden's voice. Was she interrupting something? Surely, not at 6:30 a.m. Unless, he had an overnight visitor. That wasn't likely considering they had said goodbye late afternoon, but it was possible she supposed. The thought of that bothered her more than she wanted to admit. Seeing no other cars in the driveway, Ember walked around back. She continued walking to the far side of the house opposite her property, and for the first time, noticed the fenced in stable. Sometimes she could be completely oblivious. She tiptoed through the dew-laden grass until she reached the barn doors. There, she witnessed Aiden cooing, making small talk with two beautiful horses. Not intent on frightening him or them, she cleared her throat before getting too close. Aiden turned abruptly but didn't appear surprised at her sudden appearance.

He continued feeding his friends. "Ready to run?" he casually asked.

Ember stood behind him, admiring the two horses that seemed to be enjoying meal time. "Are you up for it? If not—"

"I'm up for it, Em. Every morning, like I said. I do need to go change, but it won't take long."

"Who are your friends?"

The affectionate smile that lit up his chiseled face caused her pulse to quicken. He patted the dark horse with the white diamond on its nose. "This handsome guy is Solo." Aiden reached over to rub the coppery coat of the second horse. "This is my girl, Freedom. Solo and Freedom, meet Em." He sensed her hesitant stance, but encouraged, "Go ahead, they are gentle. You can pet them."

Ember, sent to horseback riding camp a few summers during her pre-teen years, fell in love with horses and riding in general. It had been years since she was on a horse, but the smell of the barn and the feel of the horse flesh on her fingertips ignited something she had long forgotten.

So deep in thought, Aiden's voice startled her, "Do you ride?"

"Yes," she stopped and clarified, "I used to a long time ago."

"We'll have to ride the trails one day. These guys don't get enough exercise, and it would be fun to take them out together. What do you say?"

"Sure." Realizing she was paying more attention to the horses than to her friend, she turned to Aiden, "Before we run, I was wondering about church."

Aiden hung up the buckets and brushes on the hooks opposite the stalls before turning to her, "What about church?"

"It's Sunday, and I would like to go. Do you have any recommendations?"

Aiden's heart weighted with immediate conviction. He could tell her about the church in River Springs he had come to love. He could tell her about the need for young people in the congregation and how she would fall in love with the fiery Georgia-born preacher's wife. He could share how the small community set him back on his feet after Audrey yanked the carpet of his future from underneath him. But something in him held back. Ember lived right next door to him. They would run together every morning, upon his insistence. He liked her a lot. Against his will. In a strange, platonic way, he was committed to her, but he wasn't ready to sit next to her on Sunday mornings with every family in the pew talking about a potential match.

He walked towards the house with her beside him. "I go to this tiny church in the forest." A pause followed as he spoke the next words thoughtfully, convincing himself they were truly for her benefit, "Em, you should try some of the larger churches in Ocala. It's only a few miles away, and you would probably enjoy the more modern style of worship."

"Oh . . ."

Was that disappointment he heard in her voice?

If it was, she recovered with a deep breath and bright smile. "Okay then. Is there one you would recommend?"

"Yeah, there's one that's not that far away. I'll give you the name and directions. In fact, the singles' pastor is a friend of mine. I'll text him and tell him to look out for you."

They walked into the house. Aiden directed her to the living room. "Just have a seat. It'll only be a few seconds."

Ember's heart fell with disappointment. Apparently, he didn't want her to attend his church with him. Mentally, she tried to reign in her insecurities and not let them take over her reaction. Maybe it was better for her to go to a different church, a church where she could meet more people and get connected to the community. She took a deep breath and looked around the space that matched the rest of the house. Painted a rich yellow, flanked with hard woods and rich colors, everything around her helped define her new friend—this mystery of a man. A bookshelf lined one wall, and her curiosity won as she perused the titles. Several classics, which didn't surprise her, were neatly lined up. Many works by Earnest Hemingway were lined up next to C.S. Lewis, followed by a copy of *The Yearling* and *The Phantom Tollbooth*—both personal favorites. He had all The Hardy Boys lined up in a row, which made her giggle. He didn't seem like The Hardy Boy type. A familiar cover caught her eye on the shelf below. She recognized that name, Hunt McCay. One of her new favorite fiction authors. In fact, several of his works lined the shelf. Aiden must be a fan as well. Ember loved how the author crafted words as if they were pieces of yarn knit together on the page. As she was musing about the storyline of McCay's latest release, the low rumble of a cough made her jump.

She turned, feeling like the proverbial child whose hand was caught in the cookie jar. Aiden's expression was . . . interesting. His olive skin flushed, and his eyes were darker than normal. Had something happened in the last few minutes? She placed the book back in its spot and walked towards him, putting her hand on his forearm. "Are you okay?"

They were only inches apart, close enough to share the same air. His neck was leaning down towards her and those dark orbs searched hers as if looking for something. If electricity was palpable, the six inches between them sparked like a campfire on the verge of lighting up the sky. Aiden stepped back and rubbed the back of his neck—a sign of unease she was beginning to recognize. "I'm fine. Are you ready?"

Yes. Yes, she was ready. She had to run now, to calm the anxiety-ridden butterflies unleashed in her stomach. *What on earth had just happened?* Trying to change the subject or launch any subject, she mentioned as they exited through the back door, "I'm a fan of Hunt McCay. I noticed you've got the whole collection."

By this time, they were jogging. His words were a whisper, barely audible even in the quiet of the forest. "I do."

"I was a member of a book club in Jacksonville. He was our first pick." A light laugh followed.

"What's so funny?"

"Pops participated in that book club. He was a real fan too. Odd—he never read fiction, but for whatever reason, McCay's stuff got his attention. It was an outstanding book. After that, I was hooked. I love how he uses the page like an easel."

Aiden's flushed face turned slightly. "How so?"

"He paints with his words. Layer upon layer; not only can I visualize what he is describing, but his writing pulls in all my senses. Try reading his work out loud sometimes. The rhythm of the prose is beautiful."

Aiden's pace picked up, and Ember stretched her stride to keep up. Making record time, they crossed the imaginary finish line two minutes faster than the day before. Both had to walk it off, breathing heavily. When she finally found her voice, she looked at Aiden methodically stretching. "Was the devil chasing you, Son?" Ember said with a southern drawl, and a mischievous glint in her eye.

Her question was effective in stopping him and forcing eye contact. He started laughing, a laugh that reached down deep and rumbled through the piney brush that surrounded them. Aiden walked over to the wooden steps, off the back porch, and sat down. "I haven't heard that in years."

Her grandfather's old country sayings were part of Ransom's signature vocabulary. She joined Aiden on the steps, conscious of their legs touching, but also enjoying the fact that she could sit and remember her grandfather with someone who loved him—maybe as much as she did.

"Do you have a favorite Pops-ism?" Aiden asked.

"Yes," Ember smiled. "When my dad would visit Pops after a long night of partying, he would say, 'He looks like ten miles of bad road.' For some reason, I always found that humorous, especially because it was so true." She knocked her knee against his. "What about you? Do you have a favorite?"

The corners of Aiden's mouth curved up in a way that must have been reminiscent of how he looked as a boy; and for the first time, Ember even detected a dimple peeking from his left cheek. "Yeah, I'd screw up, and he'd look at me with that look . . ."

Ember giggled, picturing the look to which Aiden referred.

"He would say, 'You better give your heart to Jesus, 'cause your butt is mine.'"

Laughter had erupted between them before Ember responded, "Yeah, I was on the receiving end of that one too."

Silence hung in the air for a few moments before Ember got up and faced Aiden. Her voice was soft and measured. "I need to get ready for church. Can you text me the address?"

Aiden nodded. "Sure."

She turned and walked away from him.

He watched, feeling instant regret, hoping she would turn back.

Aiden sat ramrod straight in the second pew from the front of the tiny community church he called home. As he listened to the "joyful noise" of the hundred-soul congregation, his mind wandered in another direction—to a church fifteen miles down the road—a church where Ember would be mingling and meeting new people her age. A church that would inevitably embrace the energetic and beautiful teacher as one of their own.

He cringed when he thought about the phone call made after he saw Ember drive off one hour after they parted ways that morning. Several rings sounded in his ear before his old friend, Brayden Lee, the singles' pastor at Chapel Community Church, answered with his peppy greeting. "Hey, man! Happy Sunday!"

"Good morning, Brayden."

"Something must be up. You've fallen off the face of civilization and landed in the wilds of Central Florida. Seriously, it's good to hear your voice, but there has to be a reason you'd call me on a Sunday morning. Ready to come out of hiding?"

Aiden closed his eyes briefly as his old friend spoke truth. Brayden was right. Before moving into his home, he had lived in a house in town, enjoyed hanging out with people his age, and socialized to a degree. Post-Audrey he had succeeded in shutting himself out of the world—until now. Now, he was opening his window—a tiny bit—for the girl he couldn't get out of his mind's eye. "Do you remember Ransom Bennett?"

"Coach Bennett? Of course, but it's been years since I've heard that name. Is he back in town?"

Rapid blinks dissipated the sting of tears. "No, he passed away last month."

Silence. "Man, I'm sorry. I know you two were close."

"Thanks. His granddaughter, Ember Bennett, has moved into the old cabin and plans to stay. She's already secured a position as an English teacher at Springs High. So, she'll be around awhile. She's asked me about churches, and I gave her directions to Chapel. Could you be there to greet her, make her feel welcome?"

"Why not your church? Y'all have a great little group out there at River Springs. It would certainly be closer."

Aiden rubbed the back of his neck, desperately trying to ease the mounting tension this conversation was creating. "I just think she needs to meet people, and a bigger church would help with that." He hated the edge of curtness in his voice, but he was ready for this talk to end. "You think you can handle making her feel at home?"

Brayden laughed good-naturedly, choosing to ignore Aiden's tone. "Man, that's what I do! I'm assuming she's single?"

Although Aiden knew the singles' ministry was Brayden's gig, he still didn't like having to answer in the affirmative. "Yes."

Innocent but well-targeted mischief laced the pastor's next question. "Pretty?"

Aiden's tone was clipped. "I'll let you make that call for yourself. Just make her feel welcome, okay? She's experienced some rough stuff and deserves to be happy."

"Whoa, buddy. I get it. No problem. I do need to know what she looks like though so I can at least pick her out from the crowd."

Before Aiden could think, the words tumbled out, "You can't miss her. Medium height, red, curly hair and green eyes. She's wearing a royal blue dress."

Aiden ignored the amused tone of his friend. "All right man, no problem. I'll take care of her." There was a pause before the pastor continued, "You doing okay?"

Aiden hated lying, but he didn't know the answer to that question. Was he doing okay? Part of him was better than ever; the other part of him felt like his insides looked like a rope tied in dozens of knots. "I'm working it out, Brayden."

A pause followed, then a thoughtful, "Don't be a stranger. You have friends who miss you."

"Thanks, Brayden. I'll remember that."

Aiden pushed the bright red button and ended the call before hopping in the shower. All he could think about was the unsettling statement; "I'll take care of her." That was *his* job.

Ember pulled into the large parking lot of Chapel Community Church, slightly nervous about walking in by herself. Many vehicles crowded the parking lot, so she felt like she might blend into the numbers. She was wrong.

As soon as she walked through the double glass doors, a visitor welcome committee met her with information about the services and small group information and then pointed her to the coffee bar for a complimentary cup. *He Brews.* Clever. She tucked the information in her purse and walked towards the entrance. The church didn't look like a church at all. The coffee bar was to the left of the visitor station, but the large foyer held rows of comfortable furniture grouped in a way that made it appealing to sit down and visit. Modern paintings of various scenes from Scripture or witty thought-provoking statements decorated the toffee-colored walls. To the right, it looked as if there might be classrooms; but on the left, it was evident a booming auditorium stood behind the multiple sets of double doors. She turned her attention back to her destination. Leaning up against the counter was a good-looking guy about her age, sandy blonde hair, brown eyes, short, muscular build. Immediately, his eyes lit up when he saw her as if he recognized her. Surprised, she stopped as he put out his hand and inquired, "Ember?"

"Yes." She looked down to make sure she wasn't wearing a name tag. "How did you know?"

"I'm Brayden Lee, the singles' pastor here. Aiden called me and let me know you would be coming."

Looking out for me again, is he? Ember smiled at the thought. "That was sweet of him. Have you known Aiden for a while?"

"Since we were kids." He winked as he turned his shoulders towards the bar. "I'll tell you all about him. Let's get some coffee first. We've got time before the service starts."

After ordering and receiving their beverages, they chose a small table near the floor-to-ceiling windows overlooking the parking lot. Ember watched as all ages milled around the favorite hangout. "This is quite a big church."

Brayden nodded, but then continued explaining in a tone filled with fervor, "Yeah, we're growing. Pastor Brad is more of a teacher than a preacher, and his style of preaching tends to attract a lot of people hungry to learn about Jesus. They want to be taught—sheesh, I'm sorry. Listen to me on my soap box and you haven't even blown the steam off your first cup."

Ember laughed lightly. "It's okay." She held up her cup. "This is number three. Confession: I'm a caffeine addict." They both laughed. "I'm glad to be here and look forward to the service. How many people are in the singles' program?"

Ember listened as Brayden described everything the church had to offer. He certainly was enthusiastic, and Ember could easily see why he made a great pastor. Praise music, wafting through the speakers, interrupted his chatter. Apparently, it signaled everyone to move together towards the sanctuary. She started to throw her half-finished coffee away, but Brayden stopped her. "You can totally bring that with you. No problem whatsoever."

Thankful for the opportunity to finish, she followed Brayden inside a large room that was more of an auditorium than a sanctuary. Her church in Jacksonville was large, but it had traditional pews, stained glass windows, a pulpit and a baptismal. This place looked like a rock concert was getting ready to take place. Brayden ushered her into a section of people who looked anywhere from college-aged to fifties. They were very friendly, but it was hard to hear over the band. She took a chair beside two girls as Brayden asked, "Will you be okay?" He touched an earpiece she hadn't noticed. "The sound booth is calling." She nodded her head, knowing words would be swallowed by the music.

Everything from the praise and worship to the prayer time was contemporary. Brayden was right about Pastor Brad. He was an excellent teacher. The sermon on a believer's foundation rooted in Jesus was solid and adhered to Scripture. With faith, one would never be alone. The reminder brought her a tremendous sense of peace. The focus verse, Galatians 2:20, was highlighted in her Bible. *I have been crucified with Christ. It is no longer I who live, but Christ who lives in me. And the life I now live in the flesh I live by faith in the Son of God, who loved me and gave himself for me.* The service ended with an invitation; the band played for several minutes after the final prayer, and the singles, of which there were many, introduced themselves. Ember knew the avalanche of names would never stick, but nevertheless, she shook at least fifty hands. Brayden asked if she could hang out for a minute until he packed up his stuff. Soon, he was walking her to her car.

"Do you have lunch plans?"

Something about him put her at ease and told her he wasn't interested beyond getting to know her as a future member of his group. Because of that, she accepted and followed him to a hole in the wall diner that boasted great soups and sandwiches.

The waitress walked away with their orders, and Brayden immediately asked, "So what did you think?"

Ember squeezed the lime juice into her glass, dunked it, and took a sip of her ice water before answering, "It was great. Loved everything from the music to the preaching—teaching. Thank you for the warm welcome."

"But . . ."

Ember raised her eyebrows. "But . . ."

"You won't be coming back?"

She could feel the color creeping up her neck. Ember didn't want to hurt his feelings, but she did intend to visit other churches and told him so.

Brayden nodded. "Smart move. You should visit around."

Ember sighed in relief. "Thank you." She looked around at the diverse crowd before asking, "So you said you've known Aiden for a while?"

Brayden laughed, which is something Brayden did a lot. A head back, no-holds-barred, kind of laugh that made everyone around him smile. "Since elementary school. He was something else then. Before Coach Bennett got ahold of him."

Ember cocked her head to the side. "Pops?"

Brayden nodded. "Yep. He coached tackle football when we were kids. Aiden didn't have much of a home, so Coach took him under his wing. Changed his life."

"What about his parents?"

Brayden shrugged. "Not much to tell. Mom was busy working and had her battles to fight. Dad was out of the picture, not sure why."

The thought of Pops pouring so much into her next door neighbor warmed her heart. He invested in others—especially her, and for that, she would be eternally grateful. His wake of influence was indeed deep and wide, as the old children's song described the love of Jesus.

The waitress put their food in front of them, and Brayden blessed it. The restaurant lived up to its reputation. The tomato bisque and grilled cheese were delicious and hit the spot. Brayden insisted on paying, much to her dismay, but she thanked him graciously. As he walked her out to her car and opened her door for her, his parting words stilled her hands.

"Tell that neighbor of yours to come out of hiding once in a while. His friends miss him."

Ember, glad Aiden had friends outside of his dog and horses, sought to confirm what she already knew. "He doesn't get out much, huh?"

Brayden stuffed his hands in his back pockets and rocked back on his heels. "No, not since—" he paused. "I'll let him share that with you in his time."

She shrugged her shoulders and nodded her head in agreement. "Fair enough."

Ember put the key in the ignition, but Brayden continued, "Also, tell him that just because he's a big time, famous writer doesn't mean he's too good for those who knew him when. That might get under his skin enough for me to get another phone call."

Ember put the car in reverse as she nodded her head. Then her foot hit the break. "Big time writer? What do you mean?"

Brayden face lit up with a crooked smile. "Ever heard of Hunt McCay?"

Aiden was at the sink, washing dishes when a knock that sounded like machine gun fire drew his attention to the front door. Quickly, he wiped his soapy hands on a towel, glanced at the table where his guests were enjoying hot coffee and pound cake topped with sorbet; but now all heads, with spoons in mid-air, turned in his direction. He stayed the pastor, his wife, and the youth minister with his hand. "I'll get it."

He opened the door and his breath caught in his throat. The words he should have spoken were paralyzed at the sight of Ember, dressed in a royal blue wrap dress that only accentuated everything he found attractive about her; but what caused his pulse to go into triple-time was the fire shooting from her eyes. He'd seen her from a distance this morning as she got in her car, but the close-up view was much more distracting.

"When were you going to tell me?" The words came out like darts, aimed and on target.

Aiden looked behind him, closed the heavy front door, and stepped out on the porch. Almost as if she had a magnet pinned to her forehead, he gravitated to within inches of where she was standing. Her hypnotic stare bore into him as he placed both hands on either side of her arms. His voice dropped to a whisper. "Tell you what?"

Briefly, she looked down at his hands, seemingly distracted, but then looked at his face with renewed vigor. "That you are Hunt McCay." She turned and walked away from him to the edge of the porch. Her hands wrapped around her waist, a gesture he recognized when she was feeling hurt or insecure. "I thought we were friends." When she turned back, he could see the tears gathering in her eyes.

That, he couldn't take. He moved closer to her, desperate to take the pain from those beautiful eyes. "Ember, we are friends. But we haven't known one another long, and I didn't want to—"

"You had the perfect opportunity to tell me when I was singing your praises to the heavens, but you chose not to. Why? Did you think I'd make you autograph all my books or turn into some ridiculous groupie? It's not like no one knows. Brayden, a complete stranger to me, shared your "secret identity" with me at lunch."

"You went out to lunch with him?"

"Yes."

"Alone?"

She stuttered, "Well, yes, but—"

Aiden started pacing up and down the length of the porch. "What else did he tell you?"

"Not much, except you have shut yourself off from the world. He didn't say why. He thought you should do that. Apparently, that's not going to happen though, because you don't trust me enough to tell me who you are."

Aiden walked over to where she was standing and towered over her, his eyes pleading with her to understand. "This is who I am. Hunt McCay is just a name. I have cut myself off, and I have my reasons. You're right. I should have told you this morning, but I didn't. Well, I didn't because . . ."

"You don't trust me." She finished his statement while staring at the pine boards of the wrap around porch.

Slowly, his index finger, with a mind of its own, found its way underneath her chin and directed her gaze up at him. "I do trust you, Em . . ." His eyes fixed on those full lips, and only inches separated him from doing what he longed to do from the moment he laid eyes on her.

A familiar voice with a distinct Southern drawl threw cold water on the moment. "Aiden, what's going on out here? Everything . . ."

The spitfire preacher's wife, Ms. Ellie, burst onto the scene but stopped short at the sight of him standing so close to Em.

"What we got here?" Five feet tall at best with a head full of wiry, once raven black, but now ash gray curls, Ellie Hamilton walked over and stood next to Aiden, apparently assessing the situation.

He looked from her to Em, and with a deep sigh responded, "This is Ember Bennett. Ember this is Ellie Hamilton—my mom."

Ember stared at the open face of the woman in front of her, but for the life of her, she couldn't reconcile Brayden's little bit of information about Aiden's background with the petite, conservative, beautiful Native American woman standing within inches of her son. Ember blinked rapidly as Ms. Ellie held out her hand. Ember immediately took it and watched as the older woman covered it with her other hand. Her grip was firm, and her hand felt like one who had worked hard her whole life.

"Well, don't just stand out here. Come on in and have some dessert with us."

Ember looked at Aiden, who by this time was holding the door open for the both of them. "Don't even try to argue, Em. You won't win. She's tiny but bossy."

Ms. Ellie had her by the hand and walked her to the door, but made sure she patted Aiden—hard—on the arm, causing him to rub it and reply with an exasperated, "Mother!"

"Now, you're Ransom's girl, huh? Loved that man," she turned, reached up and patted Ember's cheek and then proceeded to talk with her hands moving at lightning speed, "I was sorry to hear about him passing, but Lord, they had a party in glory that day, don't ya know. He saved Aiden's life. Did you know that? Have you heard the story?"

A muted Ember shook her head.

"No? Well, I'll have to tell ya and fill you in. 'Cause he also saved mine, yes, he did."

By, this time, Ember entered the dining area where Ellie enthusiastically introduced her, "Y'all this pretty little thing is Ember, but you go by—"

Aiden cut her off. "She goes by Ember, Mama."

Ember immediately looked at Aiden, wondering if he had tagged Em only for himself. Before she could process, the older gentleman stood up and said, "Buck Hamilton, ma'am. Pleased to meet you."

A huge hand enveloped hers, making her arm appear amputated at the wrist. Buck, standing, at least, 6' 6", with a muscular barrel chest, jet black hair and a long, old-fashioned handlebar mustache was quite the match for the five-foot tall fireball. His face held nothing but honesty and Ember immediately liked him. "Nice to meet you too."

The other person in the room was a young guy who looked to be even younger than her. He was short and thin, reminding her of a hipster with his style of dress and haircut, but attractive with a bright white smile that lit up the room. "I'm Austin Campbell. Happy to meet you."

Ember smiled and returned the greeting.

Aiden cleared his throat and pulled out a chair for Ember, while his mother scooted off to fix Ember's coffee and dessert. "Ember, Buck is the pastor of River Springs and also my mom's husband. Austin is the children's and youth pastor."

"You're dressed up for a Sunday, Ember. Did you go to church this morning?"

Ember looked over at Pastor Buck and smiled. She watched as Ellie sat a steaming cup of coffee and a delicious looking plate of dessert in front of her. Ember placed the napkin in her lap and picked up her fork while answering, "Yes, sir. Aiden told me about Chapel Community Church in Ocala, so I visited there this morning."

Ember looked down at her plate and missed the accusatory expressions that flew around the table.

"How'd you like it?" Pastor Hamilton asked pleasantly.

Ember looked up at the group, who all stared at her for the exception of Aiden, who was staring at his plate, moving his spoon around a soupy mixture of melted sorbet and a remnant of cake crumbs.

"I liked it. It was different from what I am used to, but that's not necessarily a bad thing."

"What are you used to, Ember, if you don't mind me asking?" asked Ellie, shooting a sharp look over at Aiden as if she'd been kicked.

"Pops and I went to a more traditional church in Jacksonville. One with hymnals and pews, that sort of thing. Not that one style is better than the other."

The Pastor threw his head back and laughed, before adding, "No, one isn't better than the other. Well, you are certainly welcome to visit River Springs anytime. We'd love to have you. It's more traditional, but we've got some truth-telling, God-honoring worship going on, even if we are small."

"Ember, some of your future students are in the youth group," he shot a stare at Aiden, who was now looking up with a resigned expression, "and they would enjoy meeting you before the beginning of the school year."

Ember took a deep breath and looked at them all with a sincere smile. "I would love to visit." She looked pointedly at Aiden. "Thank you for the invitation." She pushed her chair back and stood to leave. Aiden immediately did the same. She put her hand out towards him, stopping his movement towards the hallway. "I can see myself out. I've got some things to take care of this afternoon," she shook everyone's hand again. "I'm sorry to have interrupted. Thank you for an enjoyable chat. It was so nice to meet you all."

Quickly, she moved down the hallway, exited the house, and skipped down the steps eager to go home and think.

"Em, wait!"

She hadn't even reached her front door before she turned to see Aiden's apologetic face staring up at her.

Her tone was full of exasperation. "Aiden, don't even bother. Look, I had no right to barge in on your family. Sorry about that. My feelings are hurt. I was serious when I told you I wanted a friend, but for whatever reason, I overreacted. It's none of my business what you write or who you are. You've been kind to me, which is more than I could ever expect. It really shouldn't matter; it's just that . . ."

He hadn't moved a muscle during her speech but Ember noticed how tightly he was gripping the porch railing, one foot poised on the first step the other firmly planted on the ground. If she was going to live next door to the man, she was going to have to swallow her pride and be honest, in the process risking everything. "Did Pops tell you about Jonah?"

Aiden shook his head slightly, but his eyes were asking for more information.

"I worked with Jonah my first year teaching. We started dating. Fell in love, or what I thought was love at the time." Ember was fighting through the unexpected flood of emotion that swelled in her throat. Blinking rapidly, she continued, "He was killed, Aiden. In a car accident."

"When?"

"Just a few years ago."

Aiden moved up a step and reached for her hand, offering her comfort. She took it, allowing him to caress the sensitive spot between her thumb and forefinger. "It almost killed me, but Pops helped get me through it." Suddenly, she released his hand, walked to the opposite side of the porch, and stared at the bird feeder she made when she was a little girl, the one that Pops left hanging on the old oak tree all these years later. Finally, she turned to Aiden, who was standing in the same spot she left him. "I've known you for a very short period, but it seems like our histories are somehow intertwined. We share Pops, and that is beyond special. Honestly, Aiden, I'm drawn to you, and that scares me."

He began moving forward, "Em—I would never—"

Ember put her hand up to stop him. "Let me finish, please."

He stopped.

"There's something about you, Aiden." Her face blushed at her admission, "Something that I'm attracted to, something I'm scared to death of because I can't—" Against her will, the tears started flowing. She felt him behind her and didn't object when he shifted her shoulders and held her in his arms while she cried. She pulled away, again putting distance between them. "I cannot even imagine risking my heart again."

Aiden understood her words because they echoed what was in his own heart. Even though five years had passed since Audrey, he wasn't ready to fall head over heels in love; but he had a feeling his heart was tugging the rest of him down a rabbit hole whose unknown contents terrified him. As he'd held Ember in his arms, feelings stirred in him that were so unlike the ones he felt for Audrey. When Ember pulled away from his embrace, he was simultaneously disappointed and relieved.

"Em—I'm sorry I didn't tell you about McCay. The spotlight is not something I've ever desired, and when my first book hit the best seller's list, I wasn't ready for everything that came with it. I write because it's who I am. Do I love that other people want to read it? Yes, of course. But I would just as soon have them attribute the contents to an imaginary figure—but of course, send me the royalty checks."

His attempt at a joke fell somewhat flat but did bring a slight smile to her tear-streaked face.

That smile melted a small piece of his heart, causing him to risk the next question, "Can we move inside or onto the back porch, and I'll tell you about Audrey?"

Her eyes widened in surprise. "What about your guests?"

Aiden looked back at the house, shocked that he forgot who was waiting for him.

"You're right—I should get back. What about tonight?"

A sigh escaped her lips as her eyes focused on the forest beyond the neat line of her lawn. "Aiden, only if you want to. You don't owe me anything."

He reached for her hand and squeezed it for a brief second before dropping it. "I know, Em. I want to. I—I need to."

She nodded. "Okay, then. Tonight."

6

Facing friendly fire—that's what Aiden felt like as he walked down the hallway towards the kitchen. As expected, conversation stopped, and two pairs of knowing eyes rested on him. Thankful that the youth pastor had apparently taken an awkward cue and left, he chose his position strategically, sitting across from his mother and stepfather, unwilling to miss body language and eye contact. He knew Buck would not pry, only find humor in the situation—but his mother was another story. Aiden's head rose above the back of the chair, and he desperately wished for the days his height didn't prevent him from leaning his head back and closing his eyes.

"Well—"

Aiden put his elbows on the table; one hand poised on his forehead fingers caught in his hair, the other rubbing the back of his neck.

"What?"

"She's sweet."

Laughter bubbled up, first from his boisterous stepfather, and finally, from his mother.

Aiden was not laughing, but answered, "Sweet is not the first word that comes to mind when I think of Ember."

"Uh-huh. Then what is that word, Son?"

"Fire."

"After a history of ice, fire is not a bad thing."

His stepfather's reference to Audrey was not offensive because it rang of truth. "We're friends. I'm not ready. She's not ready. We've known one another for a week."

"You knew her when she was a child."

"I didn't know her, Mother. I saw her a handful of times trailing Pops like a devoted puppy."

"True, but you know enough about her from Pops."

"She lost someone awhile back–someone she loved. A guy—Jonah. Sounds like she was in love with him, like maybe something permanent was on the horizon. He was killed in a car accident."

His mother's eyes widened and pooled, her heart for people absorbing the pain. "Poor child."

"Yeah, so she's got some healing to do."

"As do you."

Aiden looked at his mother, then at his stepfather. He loved both of them dearly—so much his heart hurt at times. Losing Pops was a blow that knocked the wind out of him. Deep down, there was a fear of continued loss. Part of his reluctance to share his heart was because he didn't want to risk something he couldn't recover. Ember would fall into that category eventually—he honestly didn't know if he could afford to let that happen. He wasn't sure he could trust God to direct his steps on a journey that would cost him his heart.

Ember walked out of the shed and saw the back of Aiden rapping on her door. She didn't want to scare him, so she shined the flashlight in his direction. He whipped around, only to visibly exhale when he saw it was her.

"What are you doing out here at night?" He pointed towards the shed that stood twenty yards from the cabin.

Ember reached the porch steps and switched off the flashlight. He stood there, casually dressed in joggers and a t-shirt, holding a Tervis cup of ice water. The crinkle between his brows betrayed what—aggravation?

"Aiden, I own the property. I needed a tool, and it was in the shed. I brought a flashlight with me, and a gun." She pulled up the edge of her shirt to reveal a 9 mm Smith and Wesson.

His eyes never left hers. "One day next week, I want you to show me what you can do with that thing."

Ember placed the hammer, flashlight, and gun on the side table just inside the front door. Aiden closed the door behind them but then turned to see Ember with both hands on her hips, eyes dancing with anything but pleasure. "You don't believe me?"

He slowly took two steps towards her, almost as if she were an animal who didn't trust his intentions. "I believe you, Em. I need to see it for myself. It will make me feel better when I'm not here."

She sighed but nodded. He watched as she moved to the kitchen, grabbed a bright red tea kettle, filled it with water and placed it on the gas stove on high. She talked as she disappeared into the small pantry. "You know, Aiden, I do appreciate you caring, but I meant it when I said I don't want to be a burden. You have a life and a career. You don't need a ward, and I don't want to be one."

Ember almost dropped the cup holding the tea bag when she closed the pantry and turned into Aiden's chest. The scent of him was overwhelming to her senses. He bent down to coax her eyes, staring at the floor, to meet his. "Please stop. You are not a ward or a burden. I did make a promise to Pops, and I intend to keep it. I would like to do it as your friend, but even if you push me away, I will stick—from a distance if need be, but I will always be here for you."

Ember desperately tried to swallow the tears. Words would not form, no matter what she did. A nod is all she could manage, and she was grateful for Aiden's willingness to step aside and allow her to busy her hands with preparing the tea. Finally, she heard her voice whisper, "Do you want a cup?"

"No, thank you."

The whistle of the teapot tickled her ears, and she couldn't help but smile. Aiden's curiosity was evident on his face. "What?"

"I love that sound."

One eyebrow raised with open curiosity. "The teapot?"

"Yes. The whistling. It makes me happy."

She sensed his eyes on her as she poured the water over the tea bag and slowly stirred local honey into the hot liquid. Finally, she looked at him. "Ready?"

He nodded with an odd expression.

Dear God in heaven, how was he supposed to navigate this friendship when every cell in his body responded to her?

He sat in the chair, peripherally holding her in his gaze, watching as she folded her legs underneath her breathing in the steam from her peppermint tea. What was it with peppermint? He noticed she put it in her coffee and tea; she even smelled faintly of mint. She pulled her hair to one shoulder, and he noted the way her long fingers untangled the curls unconsciously. This meeting was his idea, and he needed to start the conversation, but he was content sitting with her for however long she would allow him. She coughed, and he realized minutes had probably passed. "Audrey was the first girl I loved."

He watched as her eyes found his, giving him the courage to continue.

"We met at church—not River Springs, but the church you visited this morning. There was an easiness about being with her—at first. The first date was followed by the second, and then they all ran together. Everything seemed right from the outside looking in, but deep down I knew there was a missing piece. Do you like puzzles, Em?"

Ember shook her head. "Hate them."

He laughed at the immediate, absolute answer. "Why?"

"I don't have the patience for them. And I can't stand lost pieces."

Aiden's heartbeat quickened. "Right, lost pieces. Well, my relationship with Audrey was this beautiful countryside landscape, bright with shades of blues, greens, and yellows, much like one of those Kinkade paintings hanging inside. All kinds of promise and imagination inside the well-constructed field, cabin, and sunset, but there were holes. Missing pieces."

"What happened?"

"She left me at the altar."

Aiden closed his eyes at the expected gasp.

He watched as Ember covered her mouth with her hands. "I'm sorry, Aiden."

Aiden stared into the darkness. "I'm not. I used to be. I hated her for it. But not anymore. We would have been miserable. I've forgiven her, at least, I think I have. Audrey never trusted me with her heart—and to be honest, I never really knew mine."

Ember's voice broke into his thoughts, "I don't know what would have happened with Jonah. It was just the beginning—you know. We happened so fast, and looking back, I feel like I clung to him in desperation. But I felt like I loved him—maybe I never really knew what love was. But I hate that he's gone. I hate that he died so young. He was a good man, and he could have made a real difference in this world. I miss him."

"I understand, Em."

"I know you do, Aiden. Thank you."

He looked at her, mirroring her watery eyes with his own, thankful for the moonlight but grateful for a cloak of darkness. "For what?"

"Trusting me."

"Same here, Em. So in the spirit of friendship and this newfound trust, would you like to visit church with me next Sunday?"

The laughter that sounded like Christmas bells danced through the night air. "I would love to."

His exaggerated sigh of relief was comical. "Good, because after today, I'd be facing the firing squad if you didn't visit at least once.

Ember blinked and found herself sitting between Aiden and his mother at River Springs Church the next Sunday. The last week had gone by in a blur. She'd wanted to get settled in her house and certain tasks accomplished on the property before the last weekend of July. At that point, she knew preparation for school would cause her life to go on fast forward. Her encounters with Aiden had been brief because of his deadlines and her chores, and now she felt as if she could catch her breath—if only for a moment. The distinct smell of most churches in her experience—a mix of candles, old carpet, furniture cleaner, and flowers—made her feel at home. River Springs held that distinctive quality.

Hymns sung by a cacophony of voices, young and old, brought a delightful smile on her face reminiscent of her time in the pew with Pops. Finally, Pastor Buck stood up to preach. His booming voice resonated off the walls of the church; there was no need to mic him—in this small setting or probably even in a large auditorium. He didn't ease into the sermon. Instead, he dove in and pulled the congregation into the deep end of Scripture, specifically Joshua chapter 2. The entire sermon was on the topic of trusting God. The push and pull of waiting on God and taking the initiative to move in a particular direction paralyzed many people. Pastor Buck recounted the story of Joshua sending spies into the Promised Land and encountering the prostitute, Rahab, which set a series of events in motion that would change the world. Did Joshua wait for God's direction to send in the spies? No. But God was already moving, preparing Rahab for what was to come. One particular point stood out to Ember. Pastor Buck leaned his large frame into the congregation and said, "Seek God actively as you are moving in the direction He has given you."

Pastor Buck apparently closed every sermon with the presentation of the gospel and an invitation to come forward for salvation, prayer, or membership. Ember's heart was beating out of her chest, much like it did when she made the decision to follow Christ long ago. She knew what she was supposed to do, and before she knew it, she was standing in front of Pastor Buck saying she wanted to join the church.

Pastor Buck leaned down and placed his large hands on either side of her arms, gently gripping them. "Are you sure, Child? You've only visited once, and there are many other churches in the area."

Ember looked up into his eyes and nodded, allowing the tears to trickle unchecked. "I'm positive. River Springs is where I'm supposed to be."

He wrapped her in a bear hug and prayed a sweet, brief prayer over her before directing her to sit on the front pew.

What had just happened? Aiden watched Ember move out of the pew, talk with his stepfather and take a seat on the front row. Had she joined the church? This quickly? He couldn't deny being pleased, but also scared. She was here to stay. The hymn ended and Buck motioned for Ember to join him in front of the congregation. He put his arm around her, causing her to look even tinier than she was. Aiden noticed the evidence of tears—he assumed tears of joy.

"Allow me to introduce you good folks to Ms. Ember Bennett. Ember is new to the area, but she has deep roots." He nodded as many of the congregation whispered recognition of the last name. "That's right, Ember is Ransom Bennett's granddaughter." He turned toward Ember. "I don't know if you realize this, Darlin', but your Pops was a beloved member of this congregation for many, many years. He's greatly missed." Aiden noticed the surprised look on Ember's face and quickly realized she didn't know. Buck continued, "Ember is also a new school teacher over at Springs High, so I know many of you will want to get to know her. We're gonna pass the plate, say a prayer, and then y'all come on up and hug her neck."

Ember, touched by the hundred new faces she saw up close and personal today, many of whom loved and adored her grandfather, said a repeated prayer of thanksgiving for the gift of the moment. Mr. Scruggs, the local grocer/proprietor, told her stories of Pops helping him through a tough time in his life. John, a local police officer, shared how Pops taught him life lessons and helped him grieve the loss of his only brother. Millie, best friends with the grandmother she never knew, talked of how Pops adored his wife and son, more than anyone she'd ever known. Students and parents introduced themselves. Many of the teenagers were shy or characteristically stand-offish, but Ember would talk to Brayden about assisting with youth outreach to break the ice. Finally, after an hour, she looked into the face of Aiden, who wore an unreadable expression. He gave her a friendly side hug, officially welcomed her, and then allowed his mother to move in for a huge hug and kiss, extending the invitation to lunch at their house. Ember looked at Aiden to assess his reaction; he must have known her thoughts because he nodded once. She graciously accepted and watched Ms. Ellie move to assist an elderly couple out the back door.

"Big day, Em. How are you holding up?"

She gave him a sideways glance as she walked to the pew they were sitting in and picked up her purse, Bible, and notebook. "I'm blessed, thankful, and a little surprised. I never planned to join the church today, but God gave me a definite push during the invitation, so I followed."

They walked in silence out to his truck, the one they rode together in just a couple of hours before. He opened the door for her. "I'm glad you listened."

Ember grabbed a handle to pull herself up, but looked back at him, making sure she caught his eyes. "That means something, Aiden. Thank you."

After lunch, Aiden drove up Ember's driveway intent on dropping her off and retiring to the safety of his office to sort through his emotions about the day. Her invasion into his life had made considerable advances in the last week, and he honestly felt like an old-fashioned abacus, back and forth, back and forth with his emotions.

"Thanks for the ride, Aiden."

"You are welcome." He put the car in reverse, appreciating the high color in her cheeks and the bounce in her step. "Taking a nap or do you have a list of 'to-dos' to accomplish?"

"I'm going exploring today. Pops used to take me down some of the trails, and I haven't had a chance to revisit them. I'm going to change, grab a bottle of water, and retreat into the woods for a bit."

She told him goodbye and shut the door to his truck, making her way towards the cabin as if this idea of solitary exploration would be okay with him. She wasn't asking permission, nor should she, but Ember knew how he felt about her "exploring" solo. He sighed. So much for time to process. He rolled down the window of his truck. "Hey, Em!"

She stopped dead in her tracks without turning around, almost like a teenager who just told her father she'd see him two hours past curfew. Finally, she turned on her heel and faced him with hands on hips. Aiden was slightly amused at her defensive expression.

"Yes?"

"I'll see you in ten minutes. Don't leave without me."

He shut out her protests with the pane of glass and maneuvered his way back onto his property, noticing she had already gone inside.

Quickly, he changed and climbed through the brush, determined he would accompany her on this jaunt.

Ember tried not to be frustrated, but she couldn't help it. She knew she was acting the part of a spoiled brat, holding onto her silence and stomping five feet in front of her companion with a determination that shocked even her. She enjoyed Aiden's company, and didn't mind sharing this with him, but she wasn't a child and refused to be treated like one. It was the afternoon. She was armed. She would be okay. All of these arguments fell flat at his feet when he knocked on her door. She resisted the urge to scream as she set on a path that brought back many cherished memories. Aiden's voice broke through her thoughts.

"Did I ever tell you about the time Pops cured me of my fear of the dark?"

She shook her head, keeping her eyes on the narrow, overgrown path in front of her, but said nothing.

"I was twelve and petrified of the dark. Hated it. Pops had tried to talk to me about logical fear and illogical fear, but I knew bad things happened when the sun went down. Partially from experience."

Ember looked behind her, but this time, Aiden focused on the tangled trail.

"Anyway, I was in my birdwatching stage, and he wanted to show me where he sighted some scrub jays. We found some nests and began examining them. Soon, it was dark. I started to get nervous. He could tell, but he kept distracting me with different topics; and before I knew it, I couldn't see my hand in front of my face. Then, I'll never forget the next words he said."

Ember stopped walking, turned, and waited.

"He said, 'Son, stay here and listen for five minutes and then find your way out. You can do it.'"

Ember gasped, "He didn't."

Aiden laughed despite the fear he remembered all those years back. Of course, he also knew the end of the story.

"What did you do?"

A guffaw escaped his lips. "What do you think I did? I waited, and then as quickly as I could move, found my way out of the woods."

"Where was Pops?"

"Waiting for me on the edge of the trail with a flashlight. He saw me running out and wrapped me in the biggest bear hug. I'll always remember that because it was the first time anyone besides my mother held me—anytime I'd allowed them to."

Ember could feel her eyes watering.

Aiden inched his way in front of her and began walking again, pushing aside stray branches with the stick in his hand. "I trusted Pops more than I feared the dark."

They'd been hiking for the good part of an hour without many words passing between them. He shared the story of his childhood fear to break the ice but re-telling it caused him to think of the lesson learned. He wasn't afraid of the dark anymore, but he was afraid of the darkness of the soul brought on by disappointment and hurt. Did he trust His heavenly Father more than he feared a broken heart or disappointed hopes?

"Aiden, look!"

Aiden's head swiveled and followed the direction of her finger, noticing a clearing no more than five feet wide on all sides a few yards off the trail. His eyes immediately narrowed, and he felt the waistband that held his gun. Slowly, he walked over to investigate, allowing Ember to come with him, to keep her safely within his reach and behind him. They were only a few miles from her property, and this was someone's primitive, temporary campsite. Chills went up his spine as he got the impression eyes were watching them. His head swiveled in all directions but saw no one.

"It's probably nothing, Aiden. You said yourself people squat in the woods. I'm sure it's nothing."

He looked down at her, praying that she was right. "Still, let's go back."

His hand found its way to her back, and he guided her back down the path, staying behind her to get a better view of what or whom might be lurking in the forest.

A scream followed by a gunshot rang through the woods sending a bolt of electricity up Aiden's spine as he jolted out of bed with Rusty on his heels into the night. It came from Ember's property. *Dear God, let her be okay.* He contemplated which way to go, but Rusty made up his mind for him as he watched the dog bolt towards the shed. It was one in the morning; why would she be there? Two weeks had passed since the Sunday she joined the church. Two weeks of working out, hanging out, and falling out had been the best in his life. Earlier that evening they'd had a heated discussion about her forgetting to set the alarm system he'd had installed. Her excuse of having never had one and having to get used to it might be legitimate, but it was not something he wanted to hear regarding her safety. He'd never had the responsibility of taking care of someone either, although he didn't say that to her.

All his fears culminated in possible catastrophe as he followed the barks of his dog until he was standing inside the shed. The scene waiting for him was something he would have itched to put on paper, but never in the reality of his mind's eye. Ember stood with her back to him, visibly shaking; gun pointed towards the back wall. Aiden approached cautiously; she turned sharply, only to drop the gun when she saw him and run directly into his chest. Immediately, he wrapped her in his arms cradling the back of her head, all the while looking for a dead animal of some kind. Her tears soaked his t-shirt, but he didn't care. He pushed the tangled curls back from her face, and carefully examined her for cuts and bruises. "What happened?"

I came out here to get a book out of my trunk. She looked up at him expecting a lecture. "Don't Aiden. I know it was stupid."

He only raised his eyebrows and allowed her to continue. "When I shined my flashlight, I saw movement on the back wall. I grabbed my gun and shouted that I would use it. I thought I saw it lunge, but I guess I was wrong—I don't know now. I screamed and shot. Whatever it was must have gotten out through the window."

Aiden released her and walked to the open window. He examined the ground, checking for signs of an animal, specifically a bear, foraging for food. There were none. Everything was shuffled, but otherwise untouched. A sense of foreboding crept up his spine, but he walked back towards Ember and gingerly picked up her gun, unloaded it and put his arm around her to walk back towards the house.

"It's okay. Whatever it was is gone. You're not staying here tonight, though."

"I—"

He tightened his grip on her. "Don't argue with me, Em. I have a long day tomorrow on the computer, and I won't sleep a wink knowing you're over here by yourself."

She nodded and went inside to gather a couple of necessities before walking the short distance to Aiden's.

Ember was still shaking by the time Aiden showed her the guest room and bathroom. No longer were her tremors from the fear induced by an unwanted visitor, although she was disturbed by the incident. What was it that she saw—a shadow, a piece of clothing, a face? A sliver of vision escaped her memory in a flash, and she closed her eyes tightly to force the image to come back to her mind. Could the thing have been an actual person? The smell when she first entered the shed stayed with her. Alcohol. Heavy liquor, the kind her father would drink when he went out with his buddies from school. She promised herself she would listen to Aiden and start using the alarm system. She would also be more cautious wandering around the property.

However, the host standing before her unsettled her more than she would ever admit. She understood his logic, but somehow it didn't seem right that she was in his home—at night. She trusted him, but did she trust herself?

Dressed in a black t-shirt and plaid pajama pants, barefoot, hair still damp from a quick shower, he slowly walked towards her. A woodsy smell of pine and spice accosted her senses. "I'm going to bed, Em." He kissed her on the forehead. "Don't hesitate to get me if you need me."

She nodded and watched him walk through the doorway and heard him trod up the stairs to what she imagined was his bedroom. Ember didn't think she could sleep when she closed her eyes. The day had been long, but her adrenaline was running steadily through her veins. Once upon a time when she was in counseling, she remembered the therapist taking her through breathing exercises to calm herself. She whispered a prayer and steadied herself with rhythmic inhales and exhales. The next moment of awareness ushered in the sunlight of a new day.

Aiden walked downstairs, noticing the door to the guest room slightly open. He couldn't help himself as his eyes wandered over the sleeping form in the bed. All he saw was a raised figure topped with red curls splayed over the crisp, white sheets. He forced himself to move towards the kitchen and start the coffee and a light breakfast. He knew she would be embarrassed this morning, but he was determined to put her at ease.

Within minutes, Aiden had a light repast on the counter, and the smell of fresh brew filled the air. Suddenly, his eyes shot up at the vision of his mother walking towards him with a smile on her face. He didn't hear her knock; of course, he didn't, she never did. Aiden closed his eyes in exasperation as she slowed near the guest room, peeked inside with characteristic curiosity, and then narrowed her gaze directly on him. He placed his index fingers against his lips and pointed towards the front door, evidently intent on her turning around and following him. Thank God she took his cue.

"It isn't what you think."

Ellie sat on one of the rockers and looked up at her son. "If you think that's what I think, then you don't know your mama, Son."

Aiden couldn't help but smile. She was right. She wouldn't assume the worst, placing a trust in him that he didn't deserve but tried to live up to every day. He explained the events of the previous evening to her. He also told her about exploring the forest and seeing a used campsite. Ellie stopped rocking; her open face transformed into a look of concern.

"You don't think it was an animal?"

"No, Mama, I don't."

"Lord, Son. What are you going to do?"

Aiden sat in the chair next to her. "Mama, I don't want to scare her, but I do want her to be cautious. She's capable of taking care of herself, but sometimes she's—"

"She's what?"

"Naive and impulsive. I'm hoping this will make her a little more cautious. I've installed an alarm system in the house which should make us all feel better."

Ellie nodded. "That's probably smart."

"Yeah, but only if she uses it."

Aiden had convinced his mother to leave before Ember awoke to prevent embarrassment. He was thankful for the timing because he had no sooner made it to the stove than heard her feet touch the hardwood floors. Within minutes, she stood in front of him, bright eyes fresh from a long rest. *Lord, give me strength.*

"Have a seat." He pointed to one of the stools that hugged the island. A giant cup of coffee flowed from the pot, and she watched with wide eyes as he took French vanilla creamer from the refrigerator and poured just the right amount in before gently pushing it towards her. Then, he dug around in a built-in cabinet underneath the island and handed her a pump bottle of peppermint. Sheepishly, he replied, "I stocked up."

She fixed her coffee and took a long sip before whispering, "Thank you."

Ember placed the mug on the stone countertop and started rubbing the back of her neck, stretching. "Aiden, I'm sorry about last night. It was stupid to go out to the shed that late. I won't do it again."

"No need to apologize, Em. But I am glad to hear you say that." He cleared his throat, hoping his next words would meet receptive ears. "I'd also like to go riding today. Do you have any plans?"

"I thought you had work to do."

Aiden knew he had work to do as well. Deadlines to meet, phone calls to make, emails to return. The mental file of all the work waiting for him dwarfed in comparison to the column entitled "Ember." He took a sip of his coffee, then proceeded to fix them both bagels with cream cheese. He brought out a bowl of melon and grapes and also placed that between them. Pushing breakfast across the space that separated them, he replied, "I do, but it will get done. I'd rather go riding. I want to show you some of the trails from a different perspective."

"I'd just planned a trip over to the school, but that can wait. Sure."

Ember patted the shiny coat of Freedom as she followed Aiden and Solo down a heavily wooded horse trail they accessed from the back of Aiden's property.

"How long is the trail?" Ember inquired.

"This one runs for about 20 miles either way. We're hitting it in the middle."

Ember felt as if she had landed in the landscape of a painting. Bathed in green and blue, the sights and sounds of the forest were spectacular and a sense of peace pervasive. It was still early enough where the sun wasn't torturous but only warmed her face and shoulders. Aiden's words interrupted her reverie.

He pointed towards the middle of the stretch of piny woods. "See that area?"

"Yes." The area he pointed to—a clearing that showed evidence of use but was currently vacant.

"People gather here at different times of the year to camp and live in the woods. Most are peaceful, but some are not."

Ember noted the proximity to her property. "By not peaceful, what do you mean?"

The trail had widened at this point, and they were side by side. Aiden's gaze shifted to her troubled expression. "Em, there has been all kind of mischief reported in these woods. Most people mean no harm at all; but if you're going to live out here, you need to be careful and aware."

Aggravation laced her tone, "Is that why you brought me out here today—to teach a life lesson?"

"Partly—yes. I do want to show you the beauty of the forest, the majesty of it all. But I want you to see it in the light of day so that you can be cautious in the dark of night. Make sense?"

Ember hated to admit the wisdom in his words, but he was correct. Nevertheless, she wasn't so naive to think an animal was the only thing that could have been lurking in her shed the night before.

"Lesson learned, Aiden. Now, can we just enjoy the scenery?"

"Absolutely." The next two hours were spent appreciating the loveliness of the woods, and she welcomed Aiden pointing out different breeds of birds and various wildlife.

Ember decided to risk the pleasant day to delve a little deeper into their friendship. "Can I ask you a question?"

"Sure."

"Have you always liked to write? Reading your work—the words on the page seem effortless."

Aiden pulled back on Solo, so they were riding side by side. "Yeah, I guess so. My sixth-grade teacher, Mrs. Siegel, required a journal. I wasn't great at expressing myself verbally, never really had the words. But given a pencil and time by myself, scenes, feelings, characters came alive in my head."

"How'd you get into novel writing?"

"Long story but the short version is after college I traveled around the United States writing for a travel magazine. The people I met intrigued me and many of my characters originated from conversations with strangers. Eventually, I tired of the constant going, sleeping in a different bed every few days. "

"So you came back home?"

"Yes."

"Do you ever miss it?"

"What?"

"The people, the places . . ."

He leaned slightly forward, speaking his words deliberately, "Em, I live in one of the most beautiful areas in the nation. I can say that knowing full well the truth of it. And—everyone I care about lives in about a ten-mile radius of my home."

She looked to the right, admiring the natural beauty of the forest and pondered his words.

"My turn."

She looked back at him with one raised brow. "For what?"

"A question."

"Okay."

"What made you a perfectionist?"

Her eyes narrowed. "What makes you think I am?"

"I've watched you carefully." He shrugged at her cocked head. "Call it a writer's flaw. From the way you run, to the way you make coffee, to the way you garden—watching you meticulously plan every minute detail of the next year. What drives you to be perfect?"

She sighed. "I've always wanted to be seen, you know. I guess I always felt ignored by my parents. At school, I got noticed because of my ability to do well and to please people."

"Pleasing people is important to you then?" He couldn't keep the wince from his face as he said it, reminded of Audrey's silence in pursuit of that end, but Ember wasn't Audrey and indeed expressed her opinions readily.

"It is, but I was around Pops to know that ultimately, putting that much stock in what man thinks is a flaw. I've never been one to shy away from a challenge or take on the truth; Pops encouraged those qualities and held up a mirror to my face when it came to my tendency to trade good work for favor."

"But you still strive for perfection."

She bit her bottom lip and gave Freedom an affection rub. "I guess so."

Aiden knew the next question was leading and shameless fishing, but he needed to ask it, to hear her voice affirm her security in their friendship. "With Pops gone and your mom and dad away, do you have someone, anyone you are secure enough to share your heart—even for a little while?"

Green eyes twinkled. "I do."

They were near the water now, and something in the trees caught her attention and broke the spell between them. "Monkeys!"

He blinked twice and questioned, "You trust monkeys?"

A giggle escaped her lips, and she pointed over his shoulder to a clearing. "No, monkeys. There!"

Aiden didn't look. Her twinkling fascination was enough to keep his attention. He'd seen the Rhesus monkeys many times, and besides, he needed Ember to answer the question. "Em—"

She looked up at him, and he couldn't help but notice how her slight blush brightened her gaze. "You, Aiden. Of course, I trust you." Again, he felt as if he stepped into the pages of one of his books, and for a moment wished he knew the end of this story.

7

Ember sat in Ellie Hamilton's kitchen, a cozy space in the parsonage she and her husband resided in, located behind the white-steepled church. Like her son's home, Ellie's house reflected who she was. Decorated in warm tones of yellows, reds, and oranges, Ms. Ellie's passion, warmth, and fire radiated from every corner of the classic white clapboard home topped with the tin roof. "Tell me about the people here, Ms. Ellie."

The woman who was becoming like a mother to her looked at her with a softness in her eyes. "Oh, Baby, good people live in these woods. Some of them have had some hard lives. A lot of darkness. But just like the sunlight filters through the trees and sets the whole forest on fire, so does the love of Jesus."

Ember loved Ms. Ellie's take on the world. She loved how she came to the table with no pretense or judgment. She met the people of her husband's congregation where they were and loved them completely.

"Will you tell me about you and Pops?"

Ellie patted her knee and moved to the kitchen sink to load the dishwasher. "Oh, Lordy, Emmy. Me and your grandaddy went back a long ways. Nothing romantic, you hear? No, those were never Ransom's intentions." Ellie looked back at Ember and winked.

"Although, don't get me wrong. It crossed my mind a time or two. Your Pops was a good-looking man."

Ember's mouth hung open, and she could feel herself blushing.

Ellie looked over her shoulder again and started to laugh as she rinsed several plates. Ember stood beside her and helped while listening. "Emmy, Ransom Bennett was the talk of these woods for a while. After his wife passed . . . well, there were lots of women here and in town that would have loved for him to look twice at them, including me."

"But nothing—"

"Nah, Ransom loved my boy, but not me. He loved me as a sister and pursued me for the Kingdom until I was ready to choke him, but our friendship was just that—a friendship—with a common goal."

"Aiden."

"Yes, and as you can see, we worked well together."

Ember looked down at the tiled floor and cleared her throat. "Yes."

"Ransom introduced me to the real love of my life."

Ember closed the dishwasher and sat down on one of the multicolored Shaker chairs that surrounded the farm table. "He introduced you to Pastor Buck?"

She wiped her hands on a dishtowel and sat back down across from Ember. "Yes, right after he led me to Jesus, he put me directly in the path of the new pastor."

"Oh, Ms. Ellie, do tell."

Ellie smiled like a school girl, both dimples showing. She passed a plate of fresh chocolate chip cookies across the table to Ember. "Grab one or two. This might take a while."

Ember took one heavenly bite and nodded her head, signaling her anticipation of the rest of the story.

"Ransom was after me all the time about watching after Aiden. I loved my boy and knew he could go the wrong way, especially with little supervision. I was thankful for Ransom lovin' him like his own, but I had been down the wrong path a long time and didn't know how to turn away. I'd long since quit the boozin' and druggin', but I was looking to fill a hole with other stuff—stuff that just leaked right out. I was empty, and Ransom could see it. One day when Aiden had gone over to his place fishin', Ransom invited me over and right there on that back porch of yours, I asked Jesus into my heart. Shortly after, he invited me to attend church. I did, and that's where I met Buck. Him being the new pastor and all, I didn't feel like I was good enough for him. But God had different ideas, and I'm thankful He did. So you see, Ransom did save my life, in more than one way."

Ember, a romantic at heart, itched for more details telling the love story of Ellie and Buck, but she would be patient and fill in those holes later. "Ms. Ellie, are you originally from this area?"

Ellie moved into the sitting room at the front of the house, sat on the plaid couch and patted the seat next to her. Ember, immediately feeling at home wherever Ellie was, kicked off her shoes and tucked her legs underneath. "No, I was raised in South Georgia. My mother was full Muscogee Indian and my father, half Caucasian and half African-American." Ms. Ellie's eyes filled with tears as she gazed at a sepia photograph obviously depicting her family. Ember guessed she was the little girl in the foursome of the two grown-ups and a toddler-aged boy. "My growing up years were rough. My parents tried, but I was never really accepted in school. As a result, I made a lot of bad choices I regret. One of them was Aiden's father. A poor farmer's boy who had acceptance problems of his own, our situation went from bad to worse when we were together. We barely had enough sense between us to cross the street, much less have a baby. At nineteen, I got pregnant with Aiden. My parents were furious, forced me to marry Martin, and then launched us into the world whether we were ready or not. Martin had no business with a family. He got into one evil scheme after another, until what I thought was a job offer led us to the forest. When in reality, it was a chance to get involved with some underhanded, no good stuff that eventually got him thrown into jail."

"Jail?"

Ellie sighed, her eyes returning from a thousand miles away. "Yes, thank God all that happened after he left us, but he did end up in prison for a busted drug operation. Martin died only a few years later during a fight in jail. Aiden was so angry when he found out; that's when he started acting out. He's always been ashamed of his father, but I think deep down inside he feels somewhat responsible, which is ridiculous of course."

"Why would Aiden blame himself?"

"Oh, Emmy. I was a mess before Martin left, and broken and alone afterward. Lost, I did the only thing I knew how to do. I worked and worked and worked. Ignored Aiden in the process. I think he blamed himself for my pain—my boy is under the illusion that he is responsible for other people and their choices. Your granddad helped him through that a little, but I still see that weight on his shoulders."

Ms. Ellie excused herself to go to the restroom, but her words sat with Ember, who pondered the burden Pops had unknowingly left with Aiden—her.

"This is quite a spread Ms. Mary has laid out."

Aiden smiled as he surveyed the long, picnic tables laden with the food offerings of the members of River Springs. Mary had to be at least eighty, but every Fourth of July she hosted a big "shindig" as she called it out on her property at Lake Eaton. Mary's humble home wasn't much to accommodate the large crowd, but no one cared about going inside. There was a restroom off the back porch and plenty of room to roam the property. A dock ran into the water, and several people ate in the shade of the oak trees. Creative church members had come up with multiple games that required little or no supplies. Ember laughed at the various antics as she watched Aiden easily interact with the congregation. He was easy around this group of people—almost relaxed. They lit sparklers with the children and then watched in awe as fireworks lit up the sky. Ember fanned herself with a paper plate, thinking it was at least ninety degrees and then wondered why the kids didn't swim earlier in the day but didn't say anything. She was lost in conversation with several different people when she realized it was getting late, and many were leaving. Ember and Aiden, along with his parents stayed to help clean up after everyone left. They were taking the last bags of trash out to the garbage can when Ember stopped and stared in the direction of the water.

"What is that?"

Aiden followed her eyes, then looked back at her, a slight smile indicating he knew what she was referring to, but intended to make her say it.

She punched him in the arm. "You see them. Those lights on the water. There's hundreds of them."

"Hmmm . . . what could they be?"

"Aiden, seriously? Are they left over from the fireworks or something?"

He rarely laughed at her, but his chuckles were hitting their mark. "Gators, Em."

"What?! All of them?"

"Yes, all of them."

Ember shivered and quickly made her way back toward the house.

"Hey, Em! Wait up. There's nothing to be afraid of." He'd grabbed her arm and turned her to face him.

"I'm not afraid. I don't plan to go near them."

"Like anything, you just have to be cautious around gators. Know the rules, be consistent, and you'll be fine."

They were standing close again—too close. His eyes examined her face. "Em, you've been different these last few days. Stand-offish. What's going on?"

Briefly, she shut his face out, closing her eyes. She'd tried to keep her distance from him, to give him space ever since she talked to Ms. Ellie. It wasn't fair that he was saddled with her—she had even considered moving at one point. Praying about it, though, a move didn't seem right. "I—Aiden, I'm not going to lie to you. I've kept to myself because I don't want you to feel stuck with me. You're not responsible for my well being. You've taken a lot on yourself, and I'm sure Pops meant well—but . . ."

Aiden's fingertips on her mouth stopped her words. The sensation of his gentle touch threatened to buckle her knees. "Don't, Em. Don't pull away. I promise I can handle it, and like I said before—I'll stick, even from a distance if need be." Ember swallowed hard as his head lowered to hers, but he didn't aim for her mouth, only her cheek. An act so sweet and innocent–yet lighting a fire in the pit of her stomach like she'd never felt before. Her hand immediately covered the spot as he withdrew. Together, hand in hand, they walked back to the house to join the others.

Ember had tried to give Aiden plenty of breathing space. She'd thrown herself into volunteering at the church. Preparation for Vacation Bible School was in full swing, and River Springs, a central location for many of the families in the forest, was expecting a full house. Ember was in charge of organizing and keeping track of the youth volunteers.

Today, however, was mostly prep for the teachers who would arrive the next day to arrange their classrooms. Aiden had unexpectedly joined her, but she didn't think much of it. Apparently, he volunteered his time every year.

A man she didn't recognize framed the doorway to the fellowship hall.

She nudged Aiden. "Who's that?"

Aiden looked over his shoulder and saw his mother walking toward a familiar figure. A small smile pulled at either side of his mouth as he looked back over at Ember. "That's Smoky Joe."

"He looks like an interesting character. What's his story?"

Aiden motioned for her to follow him to the hallway into the Sunday School rooms. Within seconds, they were behind the door of the Vacation Bible School prep room. Art supplies, signage, paper goods, and activities stacked in multiple neat piles surrounded them. "Help me sort out these name tags and I'll fill you in on Smoky Joe."

Ember sat across from him happily untangling what seemed like hundreds of lanyards.

"Smoky Joe got his name years ago when he mysteriously showed up at a burnt-out building. It was tragic. A young girl and her parents died in what first appeared to be arson but was later determined to be caused by faulty wiring. Smoky Joe was on the scene and immediately a suspect. No one knew anything about him. He had no identification and no ties to anyone in the area. We do know he's a Vietnam vet because he lived out at the VA home at Fort McCoy for a time but soon left there only to show up periodically in the forest. Like I said, he was cleared once the investigation findings were released. Some think he tried to go in and rescue the family, but no one knows."

She asked in disbelief, "So that's it? No family claims him?"

Aiden's eyes took on a faraway look. Admittedly, his imagination ran rapidly when it came to Joe. "Mama has come the closest to finding out the real truth. Joe carries a locket around with him, and he showed it to Mama once. I think he'd imbibed a bit on a still kept out in the woods, and that's what inspired him, but it doesn't matter. A picture of a little boy is inside the locket. Mama thinks it might have been his son."

Ember neatly bound the untangled strings together and propped her elbows on the table. Her voice dropped to a conspiratorial whisper, half teasing, half serious, "Do you think he's dangerous?"

Aiden placed the tags in a marked box and stacked them next to the other supplies. "I know this sounds strange coming from me, Em; but no, I don't think Smoky Joe is dangerous. I believe he's lost."

Aiden followed Ember's careful steps through the Long Cemetery and thought about the past week. Vacation Bible School was a grand success. Ember had worked harder than anyone he'd ever seen, throwing herself into the week with everything she could give. Her time with the youth was valuable; many of them gained a trusted rapport with the new teacher. He wanted to treat her somehow; give her a little break. After their run this morning, he brought up the idea of going to the shooting range. He had to admit, after watching her load and unload with the utmost safety and security in mind, and then nail her target repeatedly for two hours, he admired her skill and Pops' teaching ability. The man had taught him too, so he knew how tenacious the instruction was.

She turned to look at him, green eyes full of anticipation. He'd offered to hike the Yearling Trail this afternoon, and she was giddy with excitement. "How far is the hike again?"

"You choose. 3.5 or 5.5 miles, depending on which route we take."

"5.5."

Aiden turned on Highway 19 and ten minutes later they were pulling into the parking lot. Ember nearly jumped out of the car. Apparently, the famous book was not only a childhood favorite of his but also of hers.

They rambled through the Big Scrub hitting all the high points of the trail, Pat's Island, the cattle dip dating back to the 1920s, the sinkhole in the oak/hickory hammock, the old dogwood tree, and finally the Long Cemetery.

Here they walked inside the old wooden gate in silence, respectfully. Ember had been fascinated by all the sights and sounds of the forest, asking a dozen questions along the way; but when she came to the cemetery, they walked in different directions reading the stones that marked the lives of these settlers from a time gone by.

Into the birdsong, Ember commented, "It is all about the dash, isn't it?"

"What do you mean?"

"You know what I'm saying. The dash between the birthday and the day of death. All that matters is what's in between. How we live our lives. The effect we have on this world. Have we fulfilled our purpose? Will we have any regrets?"

Aiden thought about her powerful words for several minutes before walking out of the gate and waiting for her. It wasn't long before she joined him, her expression distant.

"Do you question your purpose? Your dash?"

Ember considered him a moment before responding, "Yes—sometimes."

"Why, Em? You obviously know your calling, and you seek to fulfill it in everything you do."

She shrugged her shoulders, and he noticed how she always looked to the right when she was contemplating a complicated answer. "Do I? Don't get me wrong. I love the kids. Love teaching. That's not quite what I mean—it's more of what I'm standing on. Is it the assurance that I can take care of myself–or that someone else is here to take care of me—or am I truly depending on God? Am I living out my moment to moment trusting Him for the next step? I'm not so sure about that. Anytime I see a headstone, I wonder about that person's dash. Did they take their last breath on this Earth knowing, really knowing, whose presence they were about to be ushered into?"

Mute, Aiden only listened and contemplated his dash and the box he'd drawn himself into these last five years.

"Brayden, what can I do for you?" Aiden, for the first time in years, didn't cringe at the sight of an old friend's name popping up on the screen of his iPhone.

"You answered. That's a start."

Aiden briefly closed his eyes. He deserved whatever he got at this point. "What's going on?"

"Remember how we used to bike the Withlacoochee Trail? I thought we might get a few friends together and try out the new trailhead in Dunnellon. An old friend of mine just opened up a little restaurant called The Burger Station in Hernando, and I want to check it out. Are you up for some adventure? You can bring Ember. How is she, by the way?"

Aiden rolled his eyes; it was just like Brayden to throw half a dozen questions at him at once. But he had to admit, he would like to see old friends; and he'd always loved the trail. He was curious to see the new section he'd read about on the travel sites he followed. "How far are we talking?"

"Thirteen miles one way. Are you up for it, old man?"

"You know the reverse psychology bit never worked on me, Brayden. I need to see if Ember has a bike; if not, she can borrow one of mine. Who else are you inviting?"

"John, Krista, and Faith. They've been asking about you and your new neighbor."

"What—"

"Calm down. That's not what I meant. They just want to get to know her and to see you. John and Krista met her at church when she visited. But Faith hasn't, and they'll be teaching together out at Springs High."

"All right, Brayden. But we're not a couple, just friends. So please, no awkward assumptions."

"When have you ever known me to make a moment awkward?"

Aiden hung up with Brayden's laughter ringing in his ear.

A winded, but adrenaline-pumped, Ember rolled up behind the five other early morning adventure seekers as they found a spot for their bikes in the parking lot of The Burger Station that sat just outside the Hernando, Florida Trail marker. A bit taken aback when Aiden asked her on an outing with old friends, she readily accepted especially after finding out one of the friends would be a future colleague. The group of six met at Brayden's home in Dunnellon and caravanned to the trailhead. The cycling was a bit challenging in places but otherwise extremely pleasant with the sights and sounds of the Withlacoochee River and the breathtaking canopies of trees arching over them as they pedaled along, serenaded by the songs of blue jays and cardinals.

An old gas station repurposed as a restaurant; Ember found the Americana/vintage-retro feel of The Burger Station whimsical and unique. The smell of all things delicious permeated the air as Ember felt her stomach growl in response. The group placed their orders and were soon sitting outside at cypress tables staring at the beauty of Lake Hernando. Central Florida was truly a hidden paradise as far as she was concerned. The spread of food the cute, blonde proprietor sat in front of them begged to be eaten, especially the recommendation of sweet potato fries with marshmallow dip. Ember, a lover of all things Thanksgiving, dug in and moaned in delight at the brilliance of sweet potato casserole "to-go" style.

Brayden swallowed a huge bite of the Chubby Burger before asking, "Faith and Ember, school starts in a couple of weeks, right? You getting excited?"

Ember looked at raven-haired, blue-eyed Faith and they both smiled, knowing most teachers would answer that question with a "yes and no" response. Faith spoke, "I'm excited about teaching, yes. All the other stuff, not so much."

"Ditto."

John, the police officer that was a dead ringer for the kid from the movie, *Rudy*, only taller, threw his trash away and added to the discussion, "My mom's a retired teacher. She would agree. As a cop, I feel the same way, though. Love the people, hate the paperwork."

"That's why I gig all the time. All music, no paperwork makes Krista a happy girl." Krista, a dark-skinned beauty, taught guitar by day, and played in various venues at night and at her church on Sundays.

Brayden rose his eyebrows as he looked at the silent Aiden, who seemed content to listen and not contribute. "And then we have our friend, the writer. Seems paperwork is all you do."

A quick rebuttal surprised Ember but pleased her at the same time. "You'd be wrong. I tell stories, Brayden. Is paperwork involved on the business side of it? Of course, like anything else. But the enjoyment comes from the telling of a tale, not the pen to paper portion—for me anyway."

"Well, no one can argue you are good at what you do, man. I've never finished one of your books unsatisfied."

The group echoed Brayden's sentiments, causing Aiden to blush, but say, "Thank you." The conversation shifted to the history of the area. An hour of easy chitchat had passed before they were back on their way, ready to work off what they had consumed.

Ember worked alongside Ms. Ellie preparing for the back to school outreach event the last Sunday night in July. She smiled as she watched the little lady who reminded her of a firefly light up the social hall with heaven bent energy. "Em, take those cups and plates to the kitchen for me, will ya? We'll start settin' the food up in a minute."

"Yes, Ma'am."

Being a part of the River Springs community had been a blessing. Ever since that talk on the Fourth of July, things had settled down between her and Aiden. A true friendship had formed, one not sparked by an uncomfortable chemistry, but shared interests, conversation, and laughter. She felt as if she had made a best friend, one she could confide in, and for that she was grateful. It's not that the physical attraction had disappeared, but that had become secondary.

She couldn't believe pre-planning for school started the next week. Ahead of her calendar, Ember's classroom was set up and ready to go, and the anticipation buzzed around her core like a firecracker ready to explode upon the ringing of the first bell.

"Has my mother commandeered every moment of your agenda this evening?"

Ember turned at the familiar, comforting tones of Aiden's voice. She stilled her hands and playfully placed them on her hips, lowering her voice to a teasing whisper, "Miracles never cease! He's out of his cave and alive!"

He put both hands up in mock surrender and began to speak, but she stopped his words with the palm of her hand. "I know. I know. Deadlines. Seriously, I know you're fighting against the clock. Does your smiling face among your non-imaginary friends mean you've sent your final email?"

"Yes, it does. And for the record, I've missed you."

Ember could no more control the warmth that started at her toes and rose to the tip of her head than she could her exhale of breath at his admission. She had missed him too. The last week had been a long one in the absence of his daily presence in her life. Even their runs had been postponed in the shadow of his deadline. She moved around the table within feet of where he stood. "So are you just going to stand there, or are you going to give your friend a hug?"

Within a nanosecond, she was in his arms. She counted the two heartbeats she allowed herself before moving to the other side of the table and continuing her preparation. She didn't have to ask for his help. He readily began setting out trays. They fell into an easy silence, and soon children of all ages from the community, along with their parents, started to pour in. Ember enjoyed moving around the room, introducing herself, and making newcomers feel at home. Aiden, content in the shadows, helped his mother in the behind-the-scenes preparation, but she sensed his presence. Towards the middle of the evening, she also sensed an uneasiness creep up her spine. Someone was staring at her. She turned towards the window and saw a face—a young face she recognized from one of the youth gatherings earlier in the summer. Henry Stone. She excused herself from the conversation and moved into the night air, hoping to catch him. She didn't have to look far. He was sitting on a bench outside the fellowship hall.

"Henry?"

He looked up but didn't say a word. Ember knew that Henry was troubled from the moment she met him. Sixteen years old and in the ninth grade, unkempt the majority of the time—Ellie had filled her in on some of his family history. A notorious uncle had custody of him while his father was in and out of prison. But instead of taking care of the boy—his uncle filled his time roaming the forest, supposedly tending to business that had him on the wrong side of the law the majority of the time. Henry, left to his own devices, made destructive choices leading him down the wrong path. Ember's heart went out to him as she took a seat beside him.

"Don't you want to come in? We've got refreshments and some school supplies for next week."

No words, just a quick nod of his head. Ember shifted as she noticed his continuous staring at her hands. What was it that captured his interest? Despite her sympathy and curiosity, she fought a sense of unease in his presence.

"Em?"

Both Henry and Ember startled, and looked up at the face of Aiden, whose expression showed anything but sympathy. Before she could speak, Henry took off into the forest behind the church.

Aiden followed him with his eyes and held his hand out for Ember to take it. She did not. "Aiden—"

"Everyone's getting ready to leave. They'd like to tell you good-bye."

Ember moved past him and walked back into the fellowship hall—alone.

Aiden paused before knocking on the front door of Ember's cabin. He knew she wasn't happy with him. They had a rather heated argument after the last person left the church—much to his mother's amusement. In Ellie's eyes, their passionate "discussions" were a sign of attraction that would play out in only a matter of time. Aiden wasn't so sure. He had come to care for Ember more than he had ever cared for anyone. A strong sense of protection was overpowering at times, and he struggled with keeping it in check. One thing he had learned about her in the last couple of months was that she was capable of taking care of herself but was too naive and too trusting. Henry Stone was a perfect example. Aiden couldn't control who was in her classroom, but there was something about that kid Aiden didn't trust, especially when he looked at Ember. Where Ember saw a student who needed attention, Aiden saw a threat to her safety. He swallowed and rapped his familiar knock. No answer. He knocked again. No answer. Quickly, he moved around to the back and breathed a sigh of relief when he saw the glow of the iPad lighting up her face.

"Em?"

She looked up but didn't say anything.

"Can I come in?"

"Aiden, it's late, and I've got a long day tomorrow."

"Pre-planning isn't until Tuesday."

"I'm going in tomorrow anyway."

"Please, Em. Just for a second."

He heard her sigh. "Okay."

He'd long since mastered his ability to control his attraction to Ember, but it was nights like tonight that made him question his self-control. No makeup, hair falling down her back, pajamas, and the trace of tears produced an unquenchable desire to take her in his arms. He offered up a prayer and followed her into the screened area to what had become "his" chair.

"I'm sorry about tonight."

"No, you're not."

He moved his fingers through his hair. She could drive him crazy sometimes. "You're right. I'm not sorry."

"No, Aiden, you're not. But I'm okay with that."

"What do you mean?"

"I know you're just trying to protect me, and I appreciate it. But, Aiden, you've got to trust me. You're going away for a month. What do you think I'm going to do?"

Aiden stood up and began pacing while Ember remained in her chair rocking. "It's not that I don't trust you. I don't trust other people."

"You sound like a parent. Again, I'm not a child. And I'm certainly not your child, or anything else for that matter–besides a friend. Would you be this freaked out with Brayden or John?"

"Are you kidding me with that horrible example?"

Her voice was resigned. "You don't trust my judgment."

"You trust too much too soon."

"And you don't trust enough."

Hands flew up in frustration. "Gah! Ember, can you tell me you don't get a bad feeling when you look at that kid?"

"I'll admit I do, but that doesn't mean he's hopeless."

"I didn't say he was hopeless."

"What if—"

Aiden turned around and put both hands on the arms of the rocker, looking eye to eye with her. "Don't say it." He knew she was going to confront the "what-if" of his history. What if Pops felt the same way about him? Where would he be?

Those glossy green eyes bore into him; eventually, she looked down, shrugged her shoulders and took a careful sip of what he assumed was peppermint tea. "Okay, I won't."

He sat back down. "Em, I want you to be careful while I'm gone. I don't want you to run by yourself. You can use the treadmill upstairs at my place. I want you to promise me you'll use good judgment. You're right. People do need help, and I love—I love that you want to help them. But not everyone has pure motives–not everyone thinks like you do."

Silence met his request.

"Em—"

"I promise I'll seek God's guidance and be more careful. Satisfied?"

"Not really, but I'll take it—for now."

The day before pre-planning, Ember rearranged the desks in her room for a final time before stepping back satisfied with their arrangement. An abrupt knock on the door made her jump; only the principal's secretary had been here earlier, but otherwise the halls were dark. She opened the door to an imposing figure, whose initial impression she didn't entirely trust. "Hello. May I help you?" She hated that her voice wobbled a bit.

The man in front of her was six feet tall, with dark brown hair and piercing blue eyes. Dressed in a very expensive slacks, shirt, and tie combination with a nametag that read, *Mr. Daily, Assistant Principal*, he walked in as if he owned not only the building but all who were in it.

He didn't offer any words, only perused her body from the ground up. Finally, when he met her eyes, she offered her hand. "I'm sorry, Mr. Daily, we've not been introduced. I'm Ember Bennett, the new English teacher."

His hesitance continued to unnerve her, but eventually he grasped her hand in a grip that made her feel as if she'd dipped her hand in a jar of slime. She quickly withdrew it and watched as he entered her classroom uninvited. He did a quick once over of her whiteboard, bulletin board, and seating arrangement before turning back around to face her. "Yes, Ms. Bennett. Mr. Hill told me he hired you while I was on vacation. Typically, we always interview candidates for teaching positions together before offering a job, but I guess this time he decided to forgo protocol."

His tone made his position on Mr. Hill's judgment in this matter crystal clear.

"Yes, well, I hope you won't be disappointed."

Again, his eyes dropped below her neck and roamed her, causing her to shiver. It wasn't that he wasn't attractive; he was, but he was creepy to the point where she needed to bathe. She hoped she wouldn't have to work with him too closely.

"I hope I won't be either, Ms. Bennett." He moved two feet closer, instinctively causing her to move two feet back. "I'm in charge of curriculum, so it is important that we get along well."

So much for not working with him. Maybe he was protective of the well-being of his students and disliked being left out of the hiring loop. "I'm sure we'll get on fine, Mr. Daily. I brought high recommendations with me from Jacksonville—"

He put his hand up to stop her. "Oh, I've done my homework, Ms. Bennett. I know all about your references." He waited several seconds before continuing. He leaned back on a student desk in front of where she was standing. His long legs stretched out in front of her, almost blocking her in. "I hear your grandfather left you the old cabin."

Stunned, she didn't know what to say. "You knew my grandfather?"

His eyes narrowed, and then he looked up at the square ceiling tiles and took a deep breath before exhaling. When he looked back at her, he tilted his head. She had never been this uncomfortable in her whole life. "Oh, yes. Ransom and I go way back. So do your neighbor and me."

"Aiden?"

"Yes, Aiden. Or Mr. Steele. Or Hunt McCay. Whichever identity he settles on."

There was no question whether or not Mr. Daily liked Aiden—or her grandfather. He stood up, towering over her. "You should—"

Then music to her ears came from the open door. That voice—albeit an angry one—caused her to take a deep, relieved breath. "Trip, what's going on here?"

"Who let you in, Aiden?"

"Who let me in? Dana let me in. Who do you think?"

"I'm in the middle of a conference with one of my teachers, so I'll ask you to let us be."

Ember stood a little straighter. "I wasn't aware your unannounced visit was considered a conference. Should I be taking notes?"

Aiden looked from Ember to Trip. "When did you start working here, Trip? I thought you were over at the alternative school."

"Not that it is any of your business, but I transferred during spring of last year."

Aiden looked down at his nametag. "You're the Assistant Principal?" His voice held a note of contempt and disbelief.

"That's right."

Aiden slowly nodded his head once, before turning to Ember. "You about ready?"

"Yes, let me gather my bags." She looked over at Mr. Daily. "I'm assuming we're done here?"

He leaned back on the desk and continued to stare at Aiden. "Not quite, but we'll pick up where we left off when school begins."

Aiden opened the door for Ember and watched as she settled into the passenger seat. He took his time walking around the back of his truck to steady his breathing. When he saw Trip standing over her, his mind flashed back almost twenty years ago. He did not want to re-live that day, so he hoped beyond hope Ember would let it go. He was thankful her truck's stubborn engine placed him at the right place at the right time.

Aiden settled in the driver's seat, put on his seatbelt, and chanced to look at his passenger. One look at her calm, analytical expression directed at him, and he knew he'd have to come clean. A deep sigh proceeded his request. "Okay, Ember, I'll fill you in. First, did you accomplish what you wanted to—before he came in?"

"I did."

"Good. I'm glad. I hope you're more at ease now."

"I'll be fine although that meeting did throw me off a bit."

His fingers found their way through his hair, and he stretched his right arm across the top of her seat to stretch his back. "Trip and I went to grammar, junior high, and high school together. There's not much to tell besides the fact that he's always been a jerk. So much so that Pops kicked him off the football team when he was in seventh grade."

"You're kidding?"

"Nope. And Pops never kicked anyone off. Trip just never followed rules, and never thought he had to. His parents are extremely wealthy—Trip got kicked out of the expensive private school he attended, so he ended up with the rest of us. He bullied everyone or tried. Never had too many friends unless he bought them."

"No girlfriends?"

Aiden could feel his face drain of color. "Not ever for very long."

"Why?"

"He'd use them to get what he wanted and then they were history."

"Ugh. That's disgusting. But why does he dislike you so much? What did you ever do to him?"

"Ironic, but I became the hero to his villain. Pops engrained in me to stand up for people when they were being mistreated, which always put me at odds with Trip."

"There's something you're not telling me, Aiden. I know it."

He brought his arm back to the steering wheel poised at 2:00. "You know Candy from church?"

"The pre-school teacher?"

"Yep. Well, she didn't have anything to do with Trip, couldn't be bought. It drove him crazy. We were at a party one Friday night after a game in high school. Trip had been drinking, and God knows what else. Candy had just had her heart broken by this guy from another school. Trip gave her a drink. Next thing you know I hear this scream from the bushes next to the house. She was trying to fight him off of her, but he was overpowering. I dragged him off. Ended up breaking his nose and my hand. I was in time, though—nothing happened."

"You saved her."

"No. I was just in the right place at the right time."

"But you could have looked away, not gotten involved."

"No—I couldn't."

She knew he was right.

Pre-planning was what she expected. Lots of new faces, most very friendly and excited, others ready for a new year to begin only for it to be over and another year ticked off towards retirement. Meetings lasted the duration of the morning, and they were given an hour for lunch. She went to her box and noticed she didn't have class rosters yet—everyone else had them during the last meeting. She walked to Mr. Hill's office and immediately turned when she saw him having a heated debate with Mr. Daily. "Wait, Ms. Bennett."

She couldn't ignore her principal, so she turned on her heel. "Yes?"

"There's been a change you need to be made aware of."

Ember took a deep breath attempting to calm her nerves. "Okay. What change? Does it have something to do with my class rosters? I haven't received them yet."

"Yes."

He gave Mr. Daily a stern look but nodded his head once. Mr. Daily walked to her and shoved a folder in her hand. "Your rosters, Ms. Bennett."

The smile on his face as he left the room was enough to make her skin crawl right off her body. She opened the folder and stared at the shortened list of names and then the lightbulb went on. She looked up at the older man who'd hired her. He was shuffling papers on his desk but finally made eye contact. "I thought I was teaching ninth and tenth-grade literature."

"You were, but Mr. Daily needs a remedial reading teacher and doesn't think the current teacher is suited for the position considering her seniority. She'll be taking your classes, and you will be taking hers."

"So all the prep I did this summer was for nothing?"

"No, it wasn't for nothing. These kids will still need the coursework; you'll be presenting the same curriculum in a smaller setting with different methods, perhaps."

"Special education then?"

He cleared his throat, clearly ready for this conversation to end. "No. We have special education programs. This class is for the kids who don't qualify, but need the extra assistance." He walked around his desk and looked at her with a fatherly expression. "Look, Ms. Bennett, I know this isn't what you were expecting, but I have faith you will do an excellent job with any student in your care. I have confidence in you."

Ember held it together until her classroom door shut behind her. Hot, angry tears streamed down her face. It wasn't that she didn't have the desire to work with kids who needed the help. She was a teacher at heart, after all, and her desire was to see every student have success. No, she would serve any kid who walked into her classroom with honor, dignity, and respect regardless of their IQ. In fact, the idea excited her in a way. No, she was upset about the look on Mr. Daily's face. It was the underhanded, unprofessional, deceptive way the change of plans was presented. She appreciated Mr. Hill's kind-hearted sentiments, but she wasn't stupid. She knew something else was behind this "switch" and she intended to find out what it was. Mr. Daily might be a bully, but Ember would not be a victim. Not now, not ever.

It felt good to laugh. Faith and a couple of the other English teachers came by and asked Ember to lunch. They sat at a nearby Mexican restaurant and immediately bonded over chips and salsa. As Ember blessed her meal quietly, she said a prayer of thanksgiving. She needed friends, and it looked as if God had blessed her with several. The three other teachers at the table were all in their twenties and thirties; Vanessa and Ash were married with children, but Faith was unattached like her. All were passionate about their jobs and excited about the upcoming year. They had just taken their first bite of their entrees when Faith asked, "Are you upset about the sudden switch in assignments?"

Ember swallowed her food and took a quick sip of water. She didn't want to come across as a complainer, but she quickly decided honesty was the route. "I'm not upset about teaching the remedial classes; I just wish I'd have been told a little earlier, that's all."

Ash, beautiful with a dark complexion, and bright brown eyes that held a mischievous glint, wiped her mouth but looked directly at Ember. "Well, I think it sucks."

Ember tilted her head, surprised at the passion in her voice.

Ash continued, "I'm the teacher Daily switched you with because of seniority, supposedly. Ember, I've only been here eight years, and I love my classes. I've got five years of experience with those kids and had no desire to give it up."

The blood drained from Ember's face. Upon seeing her expression, Ash reached across the table and placed her hand over hers. "I'm not blaming you. You had nothing to do with this. I'm just trying to figure out what Daily is up to."

Ember nodded, relieved. She bit her bottom lip, unsure of whether or not to ask the next question, "How was Mr. Daily to work for last year?"

The three women exchanged glances. Finally, Vanessa spoke up, "I don't know how he got the job, honestly. Unless it's because of his father sitting on the board of education. He's got the degrees, but his reputation in the county is horrendous. Maybe they thought sticking him in the forest was the best way to keep him out of sight. He was okay last year, even though he comes across as arrogant."

Their time was up, and they had to get back to school. Vanessa and Ash had gone to the restroom while Ember and Faith waited outside the door. Faith looked at Ember and said, "Be careful of Daily. Vanessa and Ash haven't seen a side of him I have."

"What do you mean?"

"He's a flirt, Ember. Especially with single ladies. He skirts the line of harassment like a tightrope walker. He knows what he can get away with and what he can't. I noticed the way he looked at you this morning. Just be careful. I don't trust him—not at all."

Open House at the high school was a much-anticipated event in the community, especially when word of a new teacher got out. Ember looked around her classroom, satisfied with the arrangement. Despite Daily's interference, she wasn't as intimidated as she had been at her other job. Whether or not that was because this was a smaller community, or because she had gotten to know many of her students through community outreach events, she wasn't sure. It could also be because she was changing. She could feel her confidence growing every day. After the initial introductions in the auditorium, the teachers were released to meet the students and parents in their classrooms. After an hour, Ember had shaken the hands of at least half of her students and their parents, which she considered a fantastic turnout. It was nearing 8:30; the last student had departed around 8:00. Many of the teachers had already left the building, ready to enjoy their last weekend before the beginning of school. Ember was just turning out the lights when a shadow in the hallway startled her. She recognized the large, slumping profile. Henry. She looked down the long hallway and noticed a member of the cleaning crew had shut the lights off. Uncomfortable in the darkness, she quickly turned the lights back on inside her classroom.

"Henry, you startled me. Come in."

She eyed the boy with a mix of caution and sympathy. Henry stood at least six feet tall. He was lean and muscular with a head full of strawberry blonde hair and dark brown, bloodshot eyes. His eyes darted around the room as he stepped inside. Ember looked behind him. "Did you bring someone–your uncle?"

He didn't speak, only shook his head.

"Well—that's okay. Let me get you some paperwork to take home with you so you can prepare for Monday." She walked to her desk and grabbed a packet that contained school supplies, rules, and a course description. Henry took the stapled stack of papers and rolled it up like a funnel. He paused as if he wanted to say something, but then stuck the information awkwardly in the back pocket of his ripped jeans.

"Henry, do you have anything to ask me? Any questions for Monday?"

He shook his head once but mumbled, "No."

"Okay, well, it's late, and I'm sure the staff needs to lock up."

Henry turned to go out the door, but before he made a left down the hallway, three words came from his mouth. Words so quiet, she barely heard them as she turned in the opposite direction towards her car. Three words that stayed with her during the long drive home. Three words she played over and over again in her mind as she tried to fall asleep. Three words she would never forget. *Be careful, Miss.*

8

Ember ran into the back of Aiden during their jog and fell right on her butt with a thump. He turned sharply to help her up, but she could tell something was wrong. He was purposefully blocking her line of vision, but why wouldn't they finish their jog like every other morning?

She pushed her way around him, and stumbled over a root almost face planting on the dirt when she saw what he was trying to protect her from. Something tied to the marker tree—a doll—with a note. Slowly, as if it were a snake, she started towards it.

"Em, no." He grabbed her arm.

She yanked it away from him but said nothing.

When she saw what it was her blood ran cold. It was her doll. A doll that had been packed away in her bedroom, inside her trunk. Sally Mae was her first doll and one she had treasured through her childhood. Long red yarn hair had been cut in an uneven, jagged pattern. Sally Mae's shiny black button eyes were torn from her head, and a horrible Joker-like smile was crudely drawn on her cloth face. The note read, "An eye for an eye . . ."

She felt Aiden pulling her away. She felt him taking the doll and the note from her. She heard him insist they go back and turn them into the police. She sensed him scanning the woods as he spoke to her. When they finally reached his backyard, he directed her towards the back porch.

"No, Aiden. I'm not sleeping here tonight. I'm sleeping in my bed."

"No, you are not, Em. It's not safe. I won't—"

She walked away while he was talking. She knew it was rude, but it was almost as if she were in shock. Who would do this? Who would hate her this much?

John took Aiden back to his office at the station and listened carefully as Aiden explained.

"Have there been any other incidents?"

"During the summer, she shot at something in the shed. Thought it was an animal, but I wasn't so sure. And then, we saw a campsite near her house. Never saw anyone, but something about it didn't seem right."

"Did you check the cabin? Does it look like someone broke in?"

"No, but I remembered an old key Ransom kept in the knothole of an oak tree out back. Believe it or not, it was there. I guess it's possible someone might have known about it."

"Who?"

Aiden shrugged his shoulders. "I don't know of anyone. Ransom used it at times. But, it's been years."

"Does Ember have enemies?"

"Absolutely not. Everyone that meets her loves her, with the exception of Trip Daily."

John stopped scribbling and sat back in his swivel chair. "What's Trip doing?"

"You know he's the assistant principal at the school she works at, right?"

John shook his head. "No, I lost track of that idiot years ago."

Aiden explained what had happened at school.

"Do you think he's behind it?"

"No, this isn't his style. He wouldn't get his hands this dirty."

"Yeah, I don't think so either."

"Then who? What about Coach Bennett? Did he have enemies?"

"John, you know as well as I do that Pops didn't pull any punches when it came to rights and wrongs. He called a lot people in these woods out over illegal behavior. Too many to count. But he was also loved."

"Yeah, he was, Aiden. If someone had it out for Pops though, Ember would be the perfect target. Especially if the guy's local and knows any history. I'll watch out for her while you are out of town. In the meantime, tell her to use that alarm system. It could be a real lifesaver."

He knew she wasn't happy with him but so be it. He rearranged his legs on the couch and fluffed his pillow. She could be the most stubborn woman on the planet at times, but there was no way he was getting any sleep with some maniac stalking her. He had removed the key from the tree trunk and secured the house, set the security system that she had forgotten to turn on for the last week, and searched the perimeter including the shed and the surrounding woods. How he was supposed to leave her, he wasn't sure. What felt like minutes passed when something jerked Aiden awake. A faint noise. A series of soft sounds coming from her bedroom. He bolted up, adrenaline rushing through his veins. He grabbed the gun he had on the table beside him, turned on his flashlight and slowly made his way to the threshold of her room. Ember. She was sound asleep and crying—not screaming as if in a nightmare, but quietly weeping. Gently, he sat on the edge of the bed and traced the side of her face with his fingers. Slowly, her eyes opened.

"Aiden?"

"You're crying."

She wiped her eyes, half asleep. "I was dreaming."

About what or whom? He wanted to ask but didn't have the courage. What if she said Jonah? Could he take it?

She sat up and reached over to turn the lamp on. He watched as she wiped her nose and eyes with tissue from the floral box sitting on the nightstand. "We—Pops and me—were kayaking down the Juniper Run. He kept repeating this verse to me over and over again. It was um . . ." She reached over to the table and picked up her Bible—Pop's Bible, flipped to the passage, then put her hand over her mouth.

"What is it, Em?"

She read aloud, "For by grace you have been saved through faith. And this is not your own doing; it is the gift of God, not a result of works, so that no one may boast." Then turned where he could see it. Next to the verse in Pop's handwriting, *EMBER.*

"Is that all that happened?"

She shook her head, still staring at the handwriting on the page, moving her fingertips over his penned words. "No, we beached on the stretch of land that you and I picnicked. He held my face and whispered, "I love you just as you are, and so does He." Then, he disappeared into the forest. I tried to go after him, but there was no way to get through—almost like a barrier. I miss him, Aiden. So bad sometimes it aches."

"Come here."

She leaned forward and allowed him to hold her, only for a few minutes.

Eight weeks into the school year and Ember was looking at Mr. Daily sitting on the back row of her classroom completing his fourth evaluation on her teaching ability. Highly unusual and somewhat aggravating was his constant presence and judgment considering she was just getting to know her students and their abilities. She could take constructive criticism, but his nonsensical remarks on her evaluations were confusing at best. Plus, there had been other verbal references to her inexperience—in front of other staff.

Later that afternoon, Ember walked to the conference room, mentally clearing her head for the meeting that was sure to be interesting at best. Henry Stone had never been tested for a learning disability, but the more she observed him, the more she was convinced Henry was dyslexic. How he'd made it this far without testing was a mystery to her—until she met the dad. Jimmy Stone, Henry's father, was out on parole and therefore present at the meeting.

Ember's experience with parent conferences was standard considering her short career, and she had met all kinds. Wealthy, yet ignorant. Poor, but extremely intelligent. So her judgment was not based on appearance, but the smell emanating from the other side of the table was overbearing. Days of grime mixed with alcohol and smoke filled the room to the point she wished she had a handkerchief to hold it up to her nose.

Of course, Mr. Daily was the administrator present during the meeting. As soon as she approached the idea of testing with Mr. Stone, he came across the table at her, stopping inches from her face causing her to almost gag.

"You calling my boy retarded?"

She looked at Henry whose eyes had been downcast the entire time, but now were looking anxiously between her and the assistant principal who did nothing, only sat unmovingly.

"I certainly am not. Henry is extremely bright. As you can see—"

"Sounds to me like you're saying he can't read! Stupid, no good—"

Finally, she shook herself out of shock and articulated her response. Her grandfather's voice came out of her. "Mr. Stone you will sit down right now, and you will not speak to me in that manner, or I will leave. If you do not want your son tested, then simply say so.

Either way, there is no need for that kind of behavior. Do I make myself clear?"

A look of surprise crept into the man's glassy, bloodshot eyes, followed by a menacing grin. "Ransom's girl, huh?" He looked over at Mr. Daily, who stared at her with narrowed eyes and a satisfied, yet condescending grin.

Henry's father barked out a sound that was more growl than anything else.

Ember gathered her belongings. "I'm finished here. Henry, I will see you in class."

"Ms. Bennett, you have not been dismissed."

Ember leveled her assistant principal with an icy stare. "Oh, but I have."

She walked back to her classroom, shaking from rage, stuck Henry's file back in her cabinet, locked it and went home.

The next morning, before the first bell, Mr. Hill called her into his office.

Ember's heartbeat was in her throat when she saw the displeased look on Hill's face. "Sit down, Ms. Bennett. Please."

She sat. "Yes, sir."

"Ms. Bennett, I have some concerns concerning your performance. We are nearing the end of the nine weeks. You have been observed—ahem—multiple times, many with unsatisfactory marks. Then, Mr. Daily reported that you left a meeting yesterday with a parent in a fit of anger. The father filed a complaint with me. Then, today—" he handed her a file and waited for her response. Henry's file. She looked up, confused.

"Where did you get this?"

"Another teacher found it in the women's restroom. Anyone could have seen it. Surely, you know it isn't acce—"

"Mr. Hill, I can assure you that I am very aware of student confidentiality rules. I locked this file up in my cabinet yesterday before I left. The only way it could've landed in any restroom is if someone took it out of the cabinet and put in there."

She liked Mr. Hill—had from the first moment they interviewed and shared their love for Florida football—but she had to steady her hands if she wasn't going to slap that condescending look off his face. "What are you implying Ms. Bennett? That someone broke into your file cabinet and placed the folder in the restroom? You have to admit that is pretty far-fetched."

Ember leaned forward and placed both hands on the principal's desk. "There is no need to break in if you have a key."

Mr. Hill's eyebrows rose, followed by an intense look of consideration. He gave a slight nod before Ember turned and exited the office.

Aiden, against every instinct he had, sat calmly on the leather couch in his office and watched as Ember, hair pulled back, face scrubbed of makeup sat with legs curled underneath her, crying as she retold the day's events. After Ember had accused Trip Daily of breaking into her filing cabinet, Mr. Hill dismissed her, but first scheduled a meeting after school with her and Trip. At the meeting, Ember confronted Daily about her suspicions and, of course, was met with righteous indignation. At that point, Mr. Hill dismissed Daily and had Ember sign a plan of action, detailing what changes needed to happen over the next nine weeks for her to keep her position at the school.

How anyone could not see through that jerk was beyond him. There had to be someway around Ember having to deal with him in his absence. "Don't you have a break coming up?"

Ember blew her nose. "Yeah, next week. When you leave. I'm taking you to the airport on my day off, remember? Why?"

He reached across and moved a curl away from her face, catching her off guard. "Come with me, Em."

Ember unfurled her legs and looked at him as if he had grown three heads. "What?"

"Come with me for your break. I'll buy your ticket. It'll do you good to get away. You could even turn in your two weeks notice. I know it sounds crazy, but say it wasn't a good fit. We can figure out the details when we get home. Then you could travel with me the whole month."

Ember put her head in her hands, then looked up and calmly stated. "Aiden, I'm not sacrificing my career for false accusations. The details happen to be my future. I've never quit anything in my life. I'm not starting now. What is this about?"

"I'm not comfortable leaving you."

"You cannot be with me all the time."

"What if I want to be?"

"What are you saying?"

"I don't know, but the thought of leaving you is driving me crazy, Ember." His open laptop buzzed signaling an e-mail. She watched as Aiden quickly scanned it, causing a scowl the likes of which she hadn't seen before.

"What's the matter, Aiden?"

Aiden snapped his faithful laptop shut and stared out the window. "Nothing—nothing," he turned but paused to stare at her knowing look and understood they would have an extremely long, unpleasant evening if he didn't come clean.

He turned back towards the window. "It was from Audrey."

"Your fiancee?"

He only nodded but corrected. "Ex-fiancee."

"What does she want? Has she ever contacted you before? Is everything okay?"

He looked at her, communicating an overwhelming response to the peppering of questions. She apologized but looked at him expectantly.

"I haven't heard from her since the letter she left on our wedding day. No, everything is not okay. She heard I was coming out West and wants to meet for dinner. One of the stops is only an hour away from where she lives. It's the last night of the tour."

"Is her husband coming?"

Aiden knew the status between him and Ember. Friends. Good friends. Best friends. The last few months had only proven they shared more than the bond created by Pops. They truly had things in common–their love for the outdoors, literature, and animals. His laidback nature was balanced by her passion and spontaneity. He had even ventured into public again, enjoying having her by his side. A friend to laugh with, a friend to share moments with . . . it had been nice. More than nice. Aiden felt his heart on the line again, but this time, more so than ever before, and it was only a friendship. *Only* a friendship. Shouldn't anything between two people start with friendship? Maybe that was what was missing between Audrey and him. The trust that can only be found in a bond based on the verb *like*, before graduating to *love*. He measured these next words against the expression that played out on her face. "She's divorced. She says she left things undone five years ago and wanted a chance to explain."

Those green eyes he adored never blinked but looked at the bookshelf lined with his life's work. She was bothered, which shouldn't have pleased him, but deep down, it did. "She said that in an e-mail?"

He took off his ball cap and ran his fingers through his hair. "Yeah, in an e-mail."

When she looked back at him, her tone was measured, "Will you reply?"

"Yes—no—maybe."

She waited, a dozen questions spanning the space between them, none of them given voice.

"I don't know, Em. I just don't know. I don't want to talk about this right now. Back to before—I'm not interested in Audrey. I'm interested in keeping you safe."

She watched as he started pacing the study, and her heart melted at the barely controlled emotion in his voice. "We don't know who keeps coming on your property, and then that stunt with the doll. You've got Daily giving you a hard time at school . . ."

Ember stood up and stopped him by placing both hands on his arms. "Stop. I know you made a promise, and God knows you've had to work to keep it, more than you were ever expected to. But I'm not running away from this. I've got to stand on my own two feet. God's been talking to me a lot lately, echoing actually, about trust. Everything I listen to, everything I read, everyone I talk to, the subject always circles around to trust. He's speaking to me through encounters, and I have to pay attention. I've trusted too many people, and not enough in Him. I know I haven't done anything wrong. I'm going to stay. And Aiden—"

She reached up and cupped his face. His eyes focused in on her lips, and as much as she may have wanted him to kiss her at that moment, she needed him to hear her more. "You cannot make everyone do the right thing. There are things, people, you can't protect me from. You're an honorable man and more of a friend that I could ever ask for or imagine. You're going to have to forgive to heal. And then, you're going to have to surrender."

"Em—"

"I'm not going with you, but I do think you know what you need to do while you are away."

Aiden lay in bed later that night replaying the conversation in his head. She'd pegged him; that's for sure. Of course, she meant Audrey. But not only her but his father as well. *His father.* The man who abandoned them for a life of addiction. The man who was stupid enough to get himself killed in prison. The man who his little boy self still loved. He couldn't control everyone, couldn't protect Ember all of the time, couldn't make people do the right thing. Pops made him memorize a verse when he was younger. He repeated the passage from 1 Peter into the darkness, "Humble yourselves, therefore, under the mighty hand of God so that at the proper time he may exalt you, casting all your anxieties on him, because he cares for you. Be sober-minded; be watchful. Your adversary the devil prowls around like a roaring lion, seeking someone to devour. Resist him, firm in your faith, knowing that the same kinds of suffering are being experienced by your brotherhood throughout the world. And after you have suffered a little while, the God of all grace, who has called you to his eternal glory in Christ, will himself restore, confirm, strengthen, and establish you."

Aiden reached into his nightstand and retrieved the worn piece of paper from its designated place—the final letter from Pops. He read it silently.

> *Aiden,*
> *I enjoyed our visit a couple of weeks ago. Thanks for coming to see an old man living out his last days. I miss you, Boy. I thank you for understanding my need to be here. I'm so proud of you, Son. Proud of the man you've become. My heart broke for you that terrible day in the church. Not because of what the girl did, but because of the expression on your face. The longing for acceptance you've always had, the one that was shattered—yet again. Remember, you are accepted by the only One who matters; and Boy, you can't control the world. You can't make everyone do right. Don't box yourself in. I see you doing it, and my heart hurts for you. You've created something beautiful out in those woods. But beauty imprisoned in fear is like shattered glass. Broken and dangerous. Trust, Boy. Remember the verse from Proverbs. You ain't going to understand everything but lean on the One who does. I've a favor to ask you. A last request. I'm sending my girl out to the woods—giving her the cabin. I know she'll come soon after I'm gone. Will you watch out for her? Maybe show her the*

> *beauty of the forest? Show her the beauty of the people. You two are my most favorite here on this planet, and as I prepare to see my Jesus face-to-face, I ask you to take care of one another.*
> *Love, Pops*

Hot tears ran down both sides of his face as he prayed, "God, You know I love You. And I want to trust You. I want to lay all this down. I'm scared. Scared of the evil in this world. Scared of what might happen if I'm not on watch. Scared of risking my heart, especially with her. Lord, I'm so flawed, so selfish at times I can barely stand myself. You know my heart. Help me not to be fearful, to embrace the life You've given me, to love others as You have commanded, and to leave the judgment to You. Thank you, Lord."

Ember hesitated at the security gate in Orlando International Airport and watched as Aiden zipped up his carry on. She could feel the emotion welling in her throat, but she was determined not to cry. They weren't dating, but she would miss him—desperately.

He tapped his index finger on her chin. "Hey."

She looked up at him blinking rapidly.

He could see her, and she suddenly felt extremely vulnerable. She watched as he placed his carry-on back on the floor of the airport. "Come here."

The step to his chest and the feel of his arms around her felt like the only home she knew. "I'll miss you."

"Oh, Em," he pulled back, willing her to look up at him, "You have no idea how much I'll miss you."

"You'll keep me posted—on everything?"

"Yes, but the tour itself is dull. It sounds glamorous, but it isn't. I'm thankful for the fans, but it's just me talking about my stories and signing books."

"I know, but that isn't everything, is it?"

"Em, I don't even know if I'll see her. I don't even know if I want to. But, yes, I'll keep you posted. Remember everything I told you about being cautious. Don't take unnecessary risks. Use that number I had you program on your phone if necessary. John is on high alert. Mom and Buck said you could go over there anytime. Don't forget that."

"Aiden, I'll be okay. You be safe."

"No, Em. You be safe."

"Ms. Bennett, can you come to my office for a moment, please?"

Ember closed her eyes and answered in the affirmative. It was 7:30 a.m. and she wanted to settle into the day, place folders on student desks, and say a prayer. Come to think of it, how did he even know she was here this early? Then she remembered the new cameras installed for security purposes. She had noticed the tech team working on them Friday after school. Apparently, Mr. Hill had watched for her this morning. What now? The long hallway was still dark and smelled of chemical cleaner and coffee coming from the teachers' lounge. The science department chair, Mr. Thibodeau, always brewed a fresh pot when he arrived at 7:00 a.m. Ember listened as her heels clicked across the cafeteria before entering the front office. She rounded the vacant secretary's desk and stopped short of Mr. Hill's open door.

"Come in, Ms. Bennett. Have a seat."

Ember did as she was told, heart beating rapidly. Was this the moment she would be released from her position? Was this the moment she'd dreaded/anticipated her whole life when someone broke the silence and said the words aloud she'd already believed about herself? *You're not good enough.*

"What I am about to tell you is confidential, but it pertains to some grievances that have been laid at your feet, so you deserve to be in the know. Mr. Daily has been terminated and escorted off the property, not to return."

Ember exhaled, the blood draining from her face. "What—what happened?"

"Without going into too many details, Ms. Bennett, we realize that the security of your filing cabinet was compromised by Mr. Daily. We have undeniable proof of that, and I now know that any observation or report of your behavior has been grievously skewed. I'm documenting this, placing a copy in your folder, and the plan we have drawn up is officially null and void."

She knew she should say something, but words evaded her. Only nodding, she got back up and walked towards her classroom, but detoured into a private teacher's bathroom and got on her knees thanking God for his grace and continuous supervision.

A knock on the other side of the door directly behind her head startled her. She opened it to find Faith's smiling face and questioning gaze. "Did he tell you?"

"How did you know?"

Faith looked down the hall slowly beginning to fill with students, then back at Ember. "Can you help me get some books out of my car?"

Ember's eyes widened and immediately caught the hint. "Sure."

When they were out of the building walking toward Faith's SUV, Ember turned to look at her friend. "So tell me. What happened?"

"Friday after school, Daily came into my room and asked some asinine question about one of my lesson plans. I'd had a long day and wasn't in the mood for his nonsense, so I challenged him. He wasn't as cool as he typically is, and apparently forgot where he was. I don't know if he'd already been questioned about you or if that came after, but I do know that he raised his voice to me and called me a name I won't repeat. Just as he reached for my arm, Mr. Hill walked in. He saw and heard enough. He apologized to me and directed Daily to his office ASAP. Next thing I know, he's being escorted off campus by security."

Ember looked at her friend in amazement. "All this happened after school on Friday?"

Faith nodded her head as she unlocked her car and grabbed a couple of notebooks, handing one to Ember. "Yep."

"I don't know whether to be horrified, grateful, or both."

"I'll make that decision for you. Both."

"Well, well . . . ain't you a pretty thing?"

Ember visibly startled when she turned toward the gravelly voice hidden behind the concrete partition at the gas station owned by one of the locals, Mr. Carlson, who attended their church. One hand had been on the nozzle, but her hand opened and released it, automatically placing it back in its holder. She leaned to the right and tried not to show her disgust at the figure who sneered at her. Years ago, she'd watched an old movie with Pops called *Cape Fear*. Robert De Niro's character gave her nightmares for months afterward, and now she was up close and personal with a blonde version of the fictional character.

"Do I know you?"

He took the cigarette butt hanging from his mouth with his thumb and forefinger and casually threw it on the ground, smashing out the embers with his foot. The irony of the action did not escape her, nor him as he continued to stare. "Naw, you don't know me, Ember. But I know who you are. Ole Man Bennett's girl. Used to see you around some when you were a little kid. Your daddy, Jase, was a friend of mine. Well, he called himself a friend, anyways."

"What do you mean by that?"

He managed to snarl and laugh at once. "That's jus' the thing; I ain't quite ready to say. I hear you're staying at the cabin. Nice place out there. Steele has kept a pretty good eye on it over the years. I hear he's outta of town."

Ember wasn't ready to give this man any information at all, and she was anxious for this conversation to end.

"You've got my boy in your class."

Ember narrowed her gaze. "Do I?"

He'd finished pumping his gas and leaned against the car, lighting another cigarette. After taking a long drag, he pulled it out and directed his beady black eyes at her person, undressing her layer by layer. "Yeah, my nephew, Henry. Me and my brother bring the boy up together after his no good ma left him. My brother said you caused quite a stir the other day at the conference. He told me you made ole Trip lose it; that don't happen often. I like gals who've got a little spunk. Makes life fun." She pulled her cardigan tighter at his suggestion.

"Ember, is this guy bothering you?"

Officer John Banner had come up behind her. Paul must have seen him the whole time, not caring whether or not he heard the insidious words coming out of his mouth. "I was just leaving, John. Thank you."

"Yeah, Officer, she was just leavin'."

"Paul, you know you ain't supposed to be smoking around the tanks. If you're done, move on down the road."

"Sure thing." He winked and tipped an invisible hat, "I'll be seeing you 'round, Em."

Ember gasped and watched as he pulled away.

9

Aiden had never envied anyone in his life as much as he did the character, Samantha, from the old television show, *Bewitched*. He wished he could wiggle his nose or wave a magic wand—anything to be home. He was tired of this tour, tired of hotels, tired of travel—but mostly, he missed Ember. He missed the way she challenged him and the way she looked at him when she dug her heels in on an issue. He missed running with her and sitting next to her as she combed long, thin fingers through her hair. He missed talking about Pops. He missed hearing her sweet voice next to him in the pew. He even missed the smell of peppermint. Aiden was grateful the book had done well; he knew his publishers were happy with the sales thus far, and he loved the enthusiasm of his fans. But there was an uneasiness in him, more so than ever before, and all he wanted to do was return home.

The assistant the PR company sent to help with signings handed him the next book with the piece of paper the fans were asked to fill out with the inscription. The black Sharpie froze in his hand when he read the words on the white slip. *To Audrey: Here's to memories made and memories lost.* He looked up into the eyes of the woman he once thought he loved, the woman who left him standing—lost and alone.

"Audrey?"

"You never returned my e-mail."

Aiden stared at the blonde-haired beauty, who once filled his heart and mind, for only a second before scrawling the requested inscription. He handed the book to her and whispered, "An hour. Starbucks across the street."

She took the book, nodded her head, and exited the crowded bookstore.

Ember was over the treadmill. Period. She knew she'd promised Aiden she wouldn't run the trail alone, but another mile going nowhere would be her undoing. It was a beautiful morning when she set out at 6:00 a.m. Her pace was faster than normal, probably due to her excitement. However, it slowed as she neared the tree that marked the 1.5-mile mark. She breathed a sigh of relief when she saw it clear of any menacing notes or signs. She'd noticed misplaced items around her cabin, but wasn't sure if was due to absent-mindedness or something more ominous. By the time, she crossed over into her yard, she'd convinced herself stress was the culprit and reinforced her self-assuredness with the non-eventful jog. She rounded the corner of the cabin, only to see a note nailed to the post. Ember's hand flew to her mouth. She tried to regulate her breathing, but the message in bright red letters sent her racing heart into triple time. *Vengeance is mine. Generation to Generation.*

"Thank you for meeting me."

Aiden huffed. "You didn't give me much of a choice. I wasn't going to debate it in front of my readers. It would be on the Internet before sunset."

Something was different about the woman sitting across from him. Her eyes, once bright and sparkling, were dead, full of what looked like regret. Her severe bob and sophisticated dress aged her, but not in a way that was negative. The set of her jaw and her wary expression told him she wasn't the same placid girl he once knew. He wanted to be happy for her, and he thought he could be—if only he knew why she wanted to talk to him after all this time.

"I'm sorry."

Aiden couldn't control the exasperated response that came out of his mouth.

"I know, inadequate for what I did, but I am sorry." She covered her hand with his, but he quickly moved it.

"I forgave you a long time ago, Audrey. Why now, though?"

"I—I've learned a lot about myself over the last few years, Aiden. I've learned that many of the problems we had were more about me than you. My marriage—if you can call it that—made me realize what a treasure you are. I know it's probably too late, but I had to try."

Aiden's mouth hung open, and no words came out. She had rendered him speechless. Did she want to get back together? Regret he expected. The apology he suspected. But a reunion—never in a million years.

"Audrey, I appreciate what you are saying, but it's too late. I'm not the same man that I was; and regardless of what you might think, I've learned that much of what was wrong with us fell on my shoulders too."

She stirred her coffee, tears evident. "We had something, Aiden. Maybe not exactly what it should have been, but something special. Is there someone else?"

Technically, no. Truthfully, yes. "There is someone, Audrey. We're only friends—good friends, but it's a friendship I cherish."

"Friendship—something we never quite achieved, right?"

"No, we didn't."

Audrey stood up and slung her designer purse over her shoulder, picked up her coffee and took a long sip before putting her hand on his shoulder. "She's a lucky girl, Aiden. I'm happy for you."

He watched as she disappeared into the crowded street and walked away—this time forever.

Ember, tired of playing the victim, would not go through another night like last night, scared of her own shadow. Aiden was due to return soon, but he wasn't tied to her. The more successful he became, the more traveling he would do. She couldn't go on acting as if she were dependent on him for her safety—no matter what he might want. No, Ember wanted answers, and she wanted them now. Henry had proven to be a good-hearted young man, haunted by shadows, but that wasn't his fault. No, she was determined in her opinion—he was in possession of a good heart with good intentions, influenced by wrong guidance. Was he trying to warn her with the cryptic note scrawled on a scrap piece of paper on her desk? She took it out of her purse and examined it again.—*Ask the goat lady.*

Who on earth is the goat lady? She could text Aiden and ask him, but she didn't want to answer any additional questions he might have. Same for Ellie and Buck. She called John and told him about the note and listened to his warnings. She begged her to let him come over and stay if she was determined to remain on the property, but she refused. And she made him promise not to text Aiden. No, she wanted to find the answer to this mystery on her own. She went to the only place she knew—Salt Haven Goods. The proprietor, Mr. Scruggs, knew everything about everyone. He'd always been kind to her when she came in for groceries, asking about the classroom and the mysterious hometown boy turned famous writer who lived next door.

She walked in and immediately took in the smell of sawdust, bleach, and old wood. The crooked smile of Katrina, whom everyone called Kat, met her at the one and only checkout lane.

"Well, hello, Missy. How you this beautiful afternoon?"

"Great, Ms. Kat. Thanks for asking. And you?"

"Right as rain, Missy. Right as rain."

"Wonderful. Is Mr. Scruggs around?"

"Oh, yeah. He in the back. Butchering up a pig, I think."

Ember swallowed before smiling. That sounded about right. "Do you think he'd mind if I went back and asked him a question?"

"Naw, Missy. He's right sweet on you. You remind him of the grandbaby he lost years ago. She was a fiery redhead too. Poor soul burned up in a fire." Kat shook her head as if pushing the unpleasant memory back. "You go on back and see Scruggs."

Ember smiled, thanking the old woman. Mr. Scruggs, a white-haired, barrel-chested man in his mid-sixties, wore a blood-stained butcher's apron and a smile as wide as the St. John's River. "Look at you, Ember. All dressed up, lookin' nice. D'you just come from the school house?"

"Yes, sir."

"Your grandfather would sure be proud of you. You're quite a sight for these old eyes."

Ember fought back tears at the mention of Pops. Oh, how she wished he was here right now.

Mr. Scruggs washed his hands and moved to stand in front of her. "You look as if you have a thought or two in that purty head, Ms. Ember. Shoot."

Ember cleared her throat. "I do have a question. This will sound strange, but do you know who the goat lady might be?"

An odd expression crossed the old man's face. "I do. What business you got with her?"

Ember had not thought this part of her story out. She stumbled through the explanation. "A student of mine—he mentioned—well, he thought I could—purchase a goat from her."

"A goat? What you want a goat for, Ember?"

She had no idea. "As a—pet."

Santa Claus's laughter could not compete with the rolling rumble of Mr. Scruggs when he threw his head back and roared. "A pet? Well, don't that beat all?"

She nodded her head enthusiastically.

"Well, I don't know about keeping a goat as a pet, but if you're looking for a goat, Ms. Abigail Destinforth, otherwise known as Destiny in these parts, lives out a ways. I warn you, Ms. Ember—Destiny is an odd one. She thinks she's part of these woods, talks to the trees and the grass, that sort. She's got goats, but Lord knows what else the woman has on that piece of property. Be careful when you go out there." He scrawled an address on a sheet of butcher paper. "Good luck and come on by when you're done or shoot me one of those texts you young people like to use instead of actual words."

Ember gratefully accepted the address but looked at him with an odd expression. "Why?"

"Cause I wanna know you made it back."

Pops had been insistent upon the fact that Ember learn to read a map and navigate without depending on technology. For that she was profoundly grateful because the voice of Siri was thoroughly disgusted with her at this moment, insisting that the location she typed in was made up. There simply was no such place—except there was. Deep in the Florida brush, miles down a dirt road, a rickety shack stood with chickens, goats, horses, mules and turkeys roaming around freely. Skinned hogs, or, at least Ember hoped they were hogs, hung from a rod that spanned the length of the southbound porch. Ember looked at her watch—5:00. She wanted to be on her way before the hint of darkness fell. Cautiously, Ember got out of her car and slowly approached the dilapidated building. The menagerie of animals on high alert sounded like a possessed See-N-Say Fischer Price toy long forgotten.

Two headless chickens spastically ran, zigzagging right for her and Ember barely missed a turkey as she hit the ground when the sound of gunfire whizzed over her head.

"What you want!"

The goat lady. A slip of a woman standing 5'7'' sporting a wild mane of curly blonde hair, dressed in old overalls, boots, and a flannel shirt was within ten feet of where she stood, shotgun firmly in place and ready for its second round of warm welcomes.

Ember remained on the ground and held her hand up to stay the woman. "I—I–mean no harm. I just want to ask you a couple of questions. Mr. Scruggs sent me."

Shotgun lowered slightly, "Al ain't got no business sending questionin' people out to my property. Didn't you see the sign, Girly?" Destiny pointed to one of at least ten no trespassing signs that were nailed to trees lining the bumpy driveway.

"Yes, I know. My name is Ember Bennett—"

"Ransom's girl?"

Ember rapidly nodded. "Yes, I'm his granddaughter."

The gun lowered all the way. *Thanks, Pops.*

"You got questions, you say?"

Ember nodded. "Yes."

"Buy a goat."

"Ma'am?"

"You got questions need answering? Buy a goat."

"But—but I don't want a goat."

"I don't want no questions."

"Can I see your goats?"

No words, only heavy steps led Ember to the back of the property, where a mountain of mattresses, lamps, clothes, toilets, lanterns, tires, and Lord only knew what else, created a barrier between Destiny's property and the woods. "Where did all this stuff come from?"

Destiny angled her head towards Ember and without expression mumbled, "Finders keepers."

Ember nodded. "Right."

As she entered a small shed, an overwhelming odor slapped her in the face. Goats. Dozens of goats. All colors. All shapes. What on earth would she do with a goat? She had to choose one of them. As if God Himself answered her prayer, a tiny spotted coffee-colored miniature goat nudged her right below the knee. Ember resisted the "Awww . . ." that almost came out of her mouth. Goat or no goat, he was adorable. "What about him?"

"Her."

"What about her?"

Ember bent down and scooped the little one up. Destiny eyed the pairing and must have given her approval. "One hundred fifty dollars."

"For a goat?"

"It's a steal."

Ember didn't have time to argue. She had no idea what she would do with this creature, but she desperately needed the information. "Can I pick her up next week? I can give you half the money today and half when I pick her up. Deal?"

Destiny grunted, but must have arrived at a fair decision. "What's your question?"

Ember put the goat down and dug into her pocket and brought out the piece of paper. She held it out for Destiny to see. "I moved into my grandfather's cabin a couple of months ago. Strange things have been left on my property, and I've even seen—someone possibly roaming around. Yesterday, I found this nailed on my porch. I was told you might know what it means."

Destiny put down the rake she had picked up upon entering the barn and held the paper out so she could read it. The woman's haunted blue eyes darted from the note to Ember's face. "You say you live alone?"

Ember slowly nodded her head.

"You ain't got no man?"

Ember didn't answer.

"Be careful."

"Do you know who wrote this note? Please."

"Yeah, yeah I know." She handed the piece of paper back to Ember. "Come on up to the house, Girl, and I'll tell you a story. One that you need to know."

Ember followed Destiny up to the screened-in back porch and through a door that was more frame than screen. Several large dogs got up from the sunken mustard-colored couch and moved into what she presumed was the kitchen. Destiny pointed to the spot where they had lain and then took a seat in a straight back chair across from Ember. The more Ember looked at the older woman, the more she realized she was once a beauty. Living a hard life shone on around her mouth and eyes, but Em sensed in Destiny's day she would have garnered a lot of attention. It was then that she noted a wedding ring. Destiny looked down at her hand.

"Died years ago."

"Oh, I'm sorry."

"Don't be."

"You wanted to tell me a story?"

"Your grandfather was a righteous man, Ember. He loved the youngins in this community and held anyone in the position to influence kids accountable to him and the good Lord. 'Bout twenty years ago, a hometown boy showed up from prison and started cooking some bad stuff out in them woods. He was selling it at the schoolhouse. Ransom caught him one day. I believe your daddy might have had something to do with it. Anyways, he did some jail time. Got out a while back, but by that time, Ransom had moved. He went about his business and had been in trouble with the law, but I 'spect he heard about you moving into the ol' place."

"Who is he?"

"Name's Paul, Paul Stone."

Henry's uncle, the man from the gas station. "How do you know he wrote it?"

"I reckon' I know my own boy's handwritin'."

Stunned, Ember's voice went up a notch as she asked, "You're Henry's grandmother?"

"'Tis a shame, but I ain't never met the boy. They've kept him away from me all these years."

Ember waited, hoping not to hinder Destiny's willingness to share.

"The boys was always wild. Their daddy was too. Ain't proud of the way they turned out. I tried to help both of 'em. But they was as stubborn as they come. Cut me off eventually, specially after their daddy died. When Henry was born, I tried to reconcile for the sake of the child, but they—"

Destiny's eyes widened as an unmistakable and unexpected emotion welled in her throat. Em didn't dare approach her, for fear of offending, but she hoped her eyes communicated sympathy.

"No mind. Ransom tried to help, but my man wasn't havin' no interference from the outside. So, they turned out bad, parceling out that poison to the babies—listen, you're Ransom's girl, and I owe that man a lot—"

"I don't understand. I thought you said your husband wouldn't let Pops interfere."

"Oh, he didn't. But Ransom showed me hope when no one else could. He also sent money, groccries and such through Scruggs. He never let on it was him, but I always knew who it was. Bottom line—my boy will hurt you if given the chance. Like the note says, he'll want revenge. It ain't the first time he's done something bad to someone round these parts."

"What do you mean?"

"Ain't got no proof, just a feeling, but Scruggs' daughter rejected him when they was in school."

"The family that burned in the house."

Destiny's hand found her mouth as if she were experiencing something awful all over again. "Be careful, Missy."

Ember was shaking when she left Destiny's property. It was past dark, and she desperately didn't want to go home alone. She answered the text she got from Mr. Scruggs asking if she had returned and was safe. *Of course* was her two-word reply. Not quite right, but not a lie either. Ember thought back on all the intrusions on her property in the last two months. The incident in the shed, the tattered doll she once cherished that she found nailed to the tree, the misplaced items in her house, the note. All from an angry man set on exacting revenge on her grandfather who had long since passed the confines of this world. What was she going to do? Go to the police? Confront him? Take everything to Buck and Ellie's? Aiden's five texts since yesterday had gone unanswered. What was he supposed to do from the middle of Texas? She rested her head on the steering wheel and prayed, "Lord, I'm lost. I know I've depended on Aiden more than I should, but ultimately You are in control. Give me wisdom. Help me know what to do next. Amen."

A knock on her window caused her to scream. Wide eyes met those of Henry's. He looked severely beaten, injured, and was crying.

Without thinking, she opened the door and immediately surveyed his bloody nose, blackened eye, and grotesquely twisted arm hanging limply at his side. "Who did this to you?"

"Get in the car, Miss. We have to go to the police—now."

He looked around the woods as if he expected another attack any minute. That got Ember's attention.

"Get in the passenger seat, Henry. Let's go."

Quickly, she slid back into her car and put it in reverse. Henry did as he was told and slammed the door. He was obviously in pain. "Henry, we should go to the hospital first."

He shook his head violently back and forth. "No, Miss. The police station."

Ember sped down her driveway and took the right towards the nearest station. She didn't have time to text or call John; she didn't even have a chance to scream when the figure ran out in front of her car. The squeal of the breaks rang in her ears as the car came to an immediate halt. Henry immediately got out of the car to confront his uncle; and to her horror, Paul Stone struck his nephew with the butt of a shotgun. Henry fell like a dishrag to the rough road. Ember frantically reached for her gun; but before she could move, Paul had grabbed a hand full of her hair and had drug her out of the car. A shot rang out before the world went black.

Aiden's heart stopped as he tried to articulate a response to what his stepfather told him. "Missing?"

After Audrey left, Aiden immediately booked a red-eye home. He had never felt such desperation in his life. Something wasn't right. Ember wasn't texting him back, which was unusual. He knew he was overreacting, but it was like God Himself was fast- forwarding his track back home. He was halfway from Orlando to Ocala when he received the call from Buck.

"Son, I'll tell you what I know, but it doesn't look good right now. Police, John included, are covering her house and the surrounding area. I wanted you to know before you got back. Your mother can't even talk she's so upset. We don't know everything, but from what I understand, Paul Stone had been trespassing on her property since before you left. Apparently, he'd left clues—even a note. A series of events led Ember to discover it was him. The boy from her class, Henry, is apparently Paul's nephew. He was trying to warn her about him, but then Paul got wind of it and beat him to a bloody pulp, almost killed him. Ember was taking Henry to the police station when Paul jumped out in front of the car and took Ember."

Every bit of energy Aiden had was divided between listening to Buck, keeping his vehicle on the road, and breathing deeply to ward off the panic rising inside of him. "I don't understand. How do you know all this? Who told you?"

"The boy rallied at the hospital and was desperate to get her some help. He told the doctors and the police."

Aiden was in shock. "They—they haven't found her?"

A long silence before he answered, "No, Son. They haven't found her, but there's a lot of blood on the scene. A lot of blood." Buck's voice cracked. "It doesn't look good."

Aiden pushed *end.* He couldn't hear anymore. Hot, angry tears streaked his face and blurred his vision. He prayed aloud, "God, please. Please don't take her from me. I know I need to trust You—trust You more than I do. I understand, but please protect her—wherever she is."

Aiden pulled up to a scene from one of the dozens of cop shows on television. Except this one was staged within twenty yards of his front yard. Police and search dogs were everywhere. He shut the door and ran over to the property he knew better than his own only to be blocked by a familiar man in uniform. "Aiden, you can't come over here."

Aiden stretched his neck and suspiciously eyed the ambulance where the blinking lights mocked him. Shock began to infiltrate his consciousness as his eyes glued to a body covered in a white sheet rolled to the back of the ambulance. "John, you have to let me through. Is—who is that?"

The officer had both hands flattened against his chest. Could he feel the thumping that threatened to bring him to his knees?

"It isn't her, Aiden. We haven't identified the victim as of yet. He had no ID on him. Took a pretty severe gunshot to the neck and head."

Aiden closed his eyes and exhaled. He. Not she. Not his Em.

"Aiden, I'll let you know what's happening. Stay—"

Aiden turned, put his hand up to silence the officer, and quickly walked to his house. They could prevent him from going onto Ember's property, but they could not prevent him from going onto his own. Within minutes, Aiden was walking down the familiar path washed in memories of mornings filled with her. He had to find her.

Only the creatures of the forest heard his fervent prayer. "God, please. Help me find her. Lead me to where she might be. I know she's Yours. But God—I—I love her. You know that. Help me."

Aiden reached the end of the path and walked around the perimeter of Ember's property. Buck said she was apprehended on the road. He would walk in that direction until he saw something—anything—that might lead him to her.

The woods were talking to him again. A brush here, a whisper there, the chorus of whistles and chirps invaded his senses. The ache in his chest had subsided when he knew the girl was out of danger. He glanced to the right and smiled. She was sleeping, her chest moving up and down, up and down—so much like that other girl he once knew. The one he couldn't save. That red hair that looked like the flames that had finally taken her. His eyes filled with tears at the remembrance of screams. He covered his ears. He knew he wouldn't let that happen again. Last night—that scream. The hair. The boy. The evil man. The same man. He was wrong to have shot him like he did, but he didn't feel remorse. No—it was time for him to go, to meet his Maker.

Ember fought against the darkness. She could barely open her eyelids against the pressure. Her head screamed, throbbing with a blinding pain she couldn't see past. Whistling—that was the sound. "Amazing Grace," the tune. And smoke. The smoke of a pipe, maybe a fire? She felt the hard ground beneath her—sifted her fingers through leaves and dirt; but as her hands moved up, she felt a blanket, some covering. Where was she? She couldn't remember past pulling up in her driveway last night. She was praying, and then Henry—the whistling lulled her to sleep as the darkness overcame her.

Whistling. Aiden heard a familiar tune echoing through the trees. He turned slightly west towards the road. He saw a faint, barely detectable trail of smoke rising into the air.

"Ember!"

Ember's eyes flew open. Aiden. Henry. Paul. She tried to sit up but couldn't. Something was wrong with her lower back, and her left leg refused to listen to her brain. She reached out her arm, startled when it touched the rough fabric of a shirt sleeve belonging to someone leaning against the tree.

"Shhh, Miss. Not long now. You'll be okay."

She knew that voice.

Ember heard someone running through the forest—far away. She could focus now, and saw the back of a figure retreating far into the woods. And then there was a hand. A gentle hand on her face, turning her face slowly towards him. She blinked and then tears clouded her vision as she choked out, "Aiden."

"Thank God. Em, Baby, stay with me, okay? Talk to me."

Aiden squatted beside her and gently laid her head in his lap. Her grip on his shirt, the sweetest sensation he'd ever felt. She was alive, and she could move. Her leg looked broken, and her face and head bruised; but she had no open gashes, no injuries that would take her away from him. He caressed her face. "Tell me how you are. What hurts?"

"My leg and my lower back. I can move my right leg." She showed him. "But not my left. My back just feels like I fell, maybe."

"Do you remember anything from last night?"

Tears started to flow down her cheeks as she nodded her head. "I remember everything. Henry—"

"He's in the hospital but okay."

He felt her heave a sigh in relief. "His uncle—Paul Stone—he's been on my property—leaving things—notes. He—"

She licked her lips. Aiden hated that he didn't have water, but hopefully, the call he just made would bring help soon. "He jumped out in front of the car. Henry tried to stop him, but Paul knocked him out with the back of a shotgun. He was badly hurt."

Aiden tried to control the anger he felt as the story unfolded. "Paul came after me. Drug me out of the car onto the pavement. I fell. And then—I heard a shot. That's all I remember. But, Aiden, someone was here—just now. I saw him run away as you came near. But I don't think it was Paul. A voice I recognized told me it was going to be okay, but I can't place it."

A sad smile found its way to Aiden's lips as he looked in the direction the man had run. "I saw him."

"Who—"

He looked back down at her face and traced the bruises with his fingertips. "Smoky Joe."

10

Ember sighed as she adjusted herself on the queen-sized bed in Aiden's guest room. She was outnumbered by everyone on their insistence that she heal over here as opposed to her bedroom. She tried to reason that upon discovering the identity of the broken body underneath the sheet was Paul Stone she was out of danger. Smoky Joe hadn't meant to kill him—or she didn't think so at least. Not that they could ask him. He disappeared into the woods forty-eight hours ago, and no one had seen him since. She prayed if they found him, he would be found innocent based on Henry's testimony that Paul meant her real harm and that Smoky had evidently interrupted a violent kidnapping. She knew, in her head, it was better for her to be here. She had broken her leg in two places and bruised her tailbone, so she had to walk with crutches. The doctor insisted she have assistance when he learned she lived alone, and she did appreciate Aiden's help. Ms. Ellie had even moved in temporarily to assist, but it still didn't feel right. This dance with Aiden between friendship and something more had to stop. It wasn't fair to either of them. She knew what she felt in her heart; but he didn't return those feelings, and her presence was hindering him from moving on. He hadn't mentioned his meeting with Audrey, but she knew he'd seen her. In the hospital, she'd overheard him talking to his mother about the awkward meeting. Deep down, she was relieved he'd seen her and shut the door on that part of his life. But she also knew that healing would inspire moving on, and Ember would not be an obstacle on Aiden's road to happiness.

A light knock on the door brought a smile to her healing face. Aiden's knock.

"Come in."

"How's my patient?"

His patient. Aiden looked devastatingly handsome this morning, dressed in casual jeans and a pullover. Freshly showered and cologned, the urge to breathe him in was irresistible; so she took a deep breath and enjoyed the moment. He sat on the edge of her bed and moved her hair off her forehead, gently touching her bruised cheek. Ember cringed, sure the sensitive spot had managed to turn awful shades of purple and yellow within the last couple of days. She must look a wreck.

"Does it hurt?"

Briefly, she covered his hand with her own. "No, it doesn't."

His eyes narrowed, communicating the lie he perceived coming from her lips. She laughed lightly. "A little bit."

"Em—I need to talk to you."

Ember knew this was just as good a time as any to talk to him too. She sat up, fluffed the pillows behind her, and leaned against the old oak headboard. "I need to speak to you, too."

His eyebrows communicated the question.

"You first, though."

"No," his voice was uneasy, "you go ahead."

"Aiden, I appreciate you taking care of me. Your family—you—have become much like my own. I love your mom and Buck and . . ." he looked at her expectantly, and she continued, "but your family isn't mine, and it isn't fair for me to step in and prevent you from moving on."

Aiden crossed his arms in front of him and eyed her like a parent would a curious child. "Oh, really? And where do you think I'm moving on to, exactly?"

She swallowed hard. "You saw Audrey, right?"

He nodded, guessing that she'd overheard the conversation in the hospital.

She confirmed what she already knew. "And that door is now closed."

"It has been closed for a while; but if you want to know if there is closure, then yes."

"Good, I'm glad. Then nothing is holding you back from getting out again, living again, seeing your friends, dati—"

Gently, he took her hand and moved his strong one over the top of it. "Em, I don't think you've given me enough credit. Don't you think I've gotten out these last couple of months? We've gone out with friends—a lot. More than I have in years."

"Yes, Aiden, but I've been a tagalong. No girl is going to pursue you with me in tow as a pesky younger sister—one that you feel you have to watch over."

Aiden's eyes darkened as his hand moved from her hand to the side of her cheek. A husky voice whispered, "You are not, nor have you ever felt like, a sister to me."

She licked her lips and watched his eyes move to her mouth. "I haven't?"

"No, Em. Never."

She waited and soon the feel of his warm lips on hers proved stronger than any pain killer the doctor could have prescribed. What started off as sweet and innocent moved to passionate in the span of a few seconds. Finally, Aiden moved away and stood up, looking at her with such longing. The idea of it caused a flood of heat to run through Ember's body.

Aiden paced the small space at the foot of her bed. *Sister.* Ridiculous. He was in trouble, though. She was in his house, mother or no mother. She was in his head—his heart. Had been since the moment he pulled into Ransom's yard. He'd watched as other men assessed the situation and attempted to work their way into her heart, but she spent most of her time with him. Could she love him? That kiss was not awkward or in any way platonic. He wasn't sure what she had with Jonah, but what he'd just experienced, he'd never had with Audrey.

She was staring at him with her fingertips touching her mouth, waiting for him to say something. He moved a chair next to her bed because he didn't trust himself to share that intimate space with her again. This time, he took both her hands in his. "Em—here's the thing. I'm a writer, so I can wax poetic for pages. But when it comes to saying stuff, I come across as an idiot."

"You don't."

"I do. So just be patient with me for a second, okay? What I'm about to say might shock you—or maybe you've already figured it out. I'm not sure. But the thing is—I love you. I'm in love with you. But if you're not ready, if there is someone still in your heart—I can wait."

Sparkling, emerald green eyes stared at him, unblinking. Tears threatened to overflow, but she bit her bottom lip and looked down at the sheet, finally blinking them away. His heart dropped to his feet, feeling like her reluctance was a sign of her not returning his feelings.

When she looked back up at him, the brightest smile lit her face, and her soft hands reached out to take both sides of his face. "I love you too."

The next kiss required no warm-up, and Aiden found himself next to her. "Em?"

She pulled away a few inches.

"Marry me?"

"When?"

Then, something he rarely did, unless he was in her presence, happened. He laughed, a sound he thought, before Ember, was lost to his imagination or confined to the pages of his books. A feeling of release and elation threatened to overwhelm him. He went from abandonment at the altar to being found by a woman who loved him so completely, she didn't say, *yes*, but instead, *when.*

"I know a guy. He'd probably do it tomorrow if we asked."

Just then the door flew open, and Ms. Ellie came in swatting Aiden off the bed. "Yes, he will. Now get off that bed, Boy, before I whip you and Ransom come down from glory to beat you with a stick."

Aiden stood, unable to take his eyes off Ember, but accusingly said, "Mama, you were listening at the door."

Ember laughed as Ellie straightened the sheets and covers before kissing her on the cheek. "Yes, I sure was. I'm going to have myself a daughter—finally. About time. Now, you rest." Ellie looked pointedly at Aiden and directed him toward the door. "Son, let's see your stepdaddy."

"What is that noise?" Ember asked, still blushing from the kiss and the turn of events.

Ellie looked from Aiden to Ember, mischief running rampant on her face. "Yes, well . . . you had a visitor of sorts earlier. Ms. Destiny pulled up in her old truck, and before I could make it down the steps—"

Ember laughed as she watched the miniature goat run past a bewildered Aiden and leap onto the bed, nestling itself beside her. A note attached to the goat's neck read, "Finders keepers. She's yours. Her name is Kisa. Look it up."

"I never officially answered your question, Aiden." Her hands moved along the animal's back, and she looked up with a glint of amusement in her eyes. "Yes, I will marry you. But only if I can bring her with me."

A cool, December day had dawned before Aiden waited for Ember to walk down the aisle at River Springs Baptist Church. The church smelled of firewood and pine. The interior looked beautiful—already rustic—but accented with Christmas greenery, white toile tied with red, burlap ribbons, and pots of white poinsettias. One bridesmaid, Faith, already stood to the left of his stepfather, dressed in a simple, chocolate brown shimmery dress. The adorable flower girl and ring bearer waited not-so-patiently in the old red wagon as anxious adults tried to keep them still during the processional. He would be forever grateful that Ember's mother and father called a truce long enough to attend the wedding, although the differences between Ransom and his son were startling to anyone who knew the former pillar of their community. Selfless and self-centered contrasted in the father-son duo. Aiden observed the vast difference between the couple's countenances on the right side of the church versus the peace-filled expression of his mother on the left side. He then looked at the table set up beside Brayden, who stood up as best man, with a picture of Pops as a tribute to the influence on them both. Aiden realized, at that moment, the grace of God had given him an opportunity to navigate this relationship in a way that was glorifying to Him. He was no better than Jase Bennett, only redeemed by a Savior who could right wrongs.

Three months had also afforded time for him and his future bride to go through pre-marital counseling with Buck. At first, Aiden was reluctant to wait, but after prayer and a couple of good "talks" with his stepfather, he realized it was a necessary step. Looking back, Aiden remained grateful for the time to get to know Ember's heart, hear her thoughts, and walk through past hurts together. With Buck's gentle guidance, Aiden and Ember held hands while laughing, screaming, crying, and making up. Brayden nudged him from behind as the bridal entry music announced the entrance of the love of his life. His breath hitched as his eyes tried to take in every detail before the tears overtook his vision. She stood a vision from heaven, carrying a beautiful arrangement of winter wildflowers, on the arm of Mr. Scruggs, who was speechless when asked to escort her down the aisle. Ember's creamy, floor-length lace dress had belonged to her grandmother and had been tailored to fit her perfectly. Her hair was loose around her shoulders, curls framing her beautiful complexion, eyes shining as she moved toward him. Finally, his hand reached out, fingers intertwining with hers. It seemed as if eternity had passed waiting for this moment; then he blinked, and the ceremony had come to an end.

Ember couldn't believe she was standing beside her husband. They had been announced and rounded the church to the outdoor reception set up in the clearing of the forest. She gasped at the perfect picture; it was exactly as she had described to Ellie and Faith, both serving as her decorating committee. Faith, a Pinterest queen, pulled together a vintage-style reception fit for a photo shoot. A variety of burlap and lace covered farm tables topped with old, brass candlesticks sat in an arrangement with mismatched wooden chairs. Rain barrels from another century had been donated and topped with old-fashioned lanterns. Mason jars containing a variety of small gifts for the guests from the bride and groom were carefully placed on each table. A stage had been constructed out of crates to hold the local band who would play tunes she and Aiden had chosen. More than anything though, Ember noticed the quiet of the moment. Not even birdsong tickled her ears. It was silent, yet she soaked in the joyous moment of complete peace.

"Are you happy, Em?" The tickle of her husband's breath met her ears.

She looked at his face, recognizing the expression of desire and concern. Ember turned into him and kissed his cheek, lingering in the crook of his neck. "My heart is full, Aiden. And I'm so thankful."

What sounded like a squeaky toy snuggled its way between them. Aiden never broke eye contact, except for the slight eye roll before looking down at their companion, Kisa, on whom someone had tied a ribbon and a bell as if she needed any help making noise.

"This goat, Em."

"I know, honey. But Freedom and Solo don't mind their new roommate."

"They don't now that I've secured her pen."

"Did you ever look up the meaning of her name?"

She stood on tip toes, her lips inches from his. "Oh, yes."

Ember felt his heartbeat underneath her hand and teased with her fluttering eyelashes. "An acronym-Knight in Shining Armor. It makes sense since Destiny uncovered a lot of the mystery for me, and she wouldn't have said a word if I hadn't agreed to buy this goat."

Aiden looked at her with a confused expression. "Kisa's a girl, right?"

Ember slowly nodded. "Yep. I don't think Destiny cares about such details."

Ember's lips met his, not giving him a chance to respond. But as the cloud of witnesses flooded the backyard reception, he started laughing against her mouth. They both doubled over, tears streaming down their faces, Kisa squeaking between them when they were called for their first dance.

Made in the USA
Charleston, SC
30 June 2016